Saint Patrick, Thomas Ogden, Saint Secundinus

The Epistles and Hymn of St. Patrick

with the poem of Secundinus, translated into English

Saint Patrick, Thomas Ogden, Saint Secundinus

The Epistles and Hymn of St. Patrick
with the poem of Secundinus, translated into English

ISBN/EAN: 9783337300159

Printed in Europe, USA, Canada, Australia, Japan

Cover: Foto ©Andreas Hilbeck / pixelio.de

More available books at **www.hansebooks.com**

THE

EPISTLES AND HYMN

OF

SAINT PATRICK,

WITH

THE POEM OF SECUNDINUS,

TRANSLATED INTO ENGLISH.

EDITED BY

REV. THOMAS OLDEN, B.A.,

MEMBER OF THE ROYAL IRISH ACADEMY.
VICAR OF BALLYCLOUGH.

"On y voit beaucoup le caractere de St. Paul. Il possedoit assuré-
ment fort bien l'Ecriture."—TILLEMONT.

"He conquered by steadfastness of faith, by glowing zeal, and by
the attractive power of love."—NEANDER.

DUBLIN:

HODGES, FOSTER, & CO., GRAFTON STREET,

Publishers to the University.

1876.

CONTENTS.

———

EDITOR'S NOTE.

THE EDITOR is indebted to the Rev. T. O. Mahony, Professor of Irish in Trinity College, for several extracts from works not accessible in the country; and his special thanks are due to the Very Rev. W. Reeves, D.D., Dean of Armagh, for his kindness in reading over the proof sheets, and offering many valuable suggestions and corrections.

PREFACE.

Of the two letters of St. Patrick contained in this work the *Confessio* was translated and published by the editor · in the year 1853, and thus, for the first time, placed within the reach of the general public.[1] In now bringing out a new edition of it, he has been induced to include the letter to Coroticus[2] and the Irish Hymn, which comprise the remaining works of St. Patrick now extant: it seemed also desirable to add the Poem of Secundinus, the nephew and companion of St. Patrick, which contains a most interesting description of him as a missionary.

In giving faithful translations of these documents, with notes, the editor believes that he has adopted the surest method of enabling the Irish people to learn the true character of one who has been grievously misrepresented. The genuineness of these Epistles is admitted by the highest authorities,[3] and may be regarded

[1] It has been since translated by a Roman Catholic clergyman, Archdeacon Hamilton; (Dublin: O'Reilly, 1859;) by R. Steele Nicholson, (Dublin: M'Glashan, 1868,) who gives the originals; and by Miss Cusack, whose work will be noticed hereafter.

[2] A previous epistle to Coroticus is mentioned, see epistle to Coroticus, sec. 2, but is not now known to exist.

[3] Dr. Todd mentions Ussher, Ware, Cave, Spelman, Tillemont, Mabillon, D'Achery, Martene, Du Cange, Bollandus, Dupin, O'Conor, Lanigan, and Villanueva.

B

as unquestioned. They are both contained in a manuscript in the Cottonian Library, and in two manuscripts
formerly in Salisbury, but now in the Bodleian Library.
The Confessio is also found in the Book of Armagh,[4] a
compilation of the earlier part of the ninth century.

They have been frequently printed in the original
Latin: first by Sir J. Ware,[5] from the four MSS. men-
tioned ; by the Bollandists[6] from one in the Abbey of
St. Vaast at Noialle, said to be no longer in existence ;
and by Dr. O'Conor,[7] from the Cotton MS. collated with
Ware's edition, by J. L. Villanueva, and others.

In Miss Cusack's "Life of St. Patrick," the Latin
text, with collation of MSS., is elaborately given.

The text used in the present edition is that of Dr.
O'Conor, compared with the Book of Armagh, as given
in Sir W. Betham's Antiquarian Researches, and with
the edition of Villanueva.

The Irish Hymn[8] was first published by Dr. Petrie,

---

[4] This copy of the Confessio is shorter than those in the other
MSS., and this has suggested the thought that the additional matter in
them may be interpolated. A critical examination, however, goes far
to prove that this copy is really an abridgment of the original work,
the MS. from which it was copied having been in many places defective and illegible, as the marginal notes prove.—See St. Patrick,
Apostle of Ireland ; a Memoir of his Life and Mission, by J. H. Todd,
D.D., Dublin, 1864, p. 348.

[5] Opuscula. Patricii, London, 1656.

[6] Acta Sanctorum at March 17.

[7] Rerum Hibernicarum Scriptores, vol. I., Proleg., pt. i., p. cvii.

[8] *Canticum Scotticum.* It is also known as the Luireach Phadruig,
(Lorica Patricii,) the breastplate or armour of St. Patrick, and by the
name of *Fedh Fiadha*, usually translated, "The instruction of the deer ;"
but Mr. Stokes gives the correct form of the name as *Faed Fiada*,
"Guard's Cry," (Goidelica, 2nd ed. p. 151,) the word Scotticum applied to this Hymn is derived from the name Scotia, which belonged

in his essay on Tara Hill, from the Book of Hymns of
the ancient Irish Church, a manuscript which is regarded by that writer as belonging to the ninth or tenth
century,[9] and which is at any rate not less than seven
hundred years old. We have further the still earlier
evidence of Tirechan,[1] who wrote in the seventh century, that it was then certainly believed to be the composition of St. Patrick.

The internal evidence bears out this statement;
the Hymn is written in a very ancient dialect of the
Irish language; its style corresponds with that of the
Confessio, as far as a comparison can be made between
different languages; it alludes to Paganism as still pre-
valent, and it mentions no doctrine or practice of the
Church that is not known to have existed before the
fifth century. The translation is that of Mr. Whitley
Stokes, in the second edition of his Goidelica.[2]

The Alphabetical Hymn of Secundinus or Sechnall,
so-called because the stanzas begin with the successive
letters of the alphabet, is also preserved in the Book of
Hymns, and is mentioned by Tirechan in the same
passage as the Irish Hymn; there is therefore the same
evidence for its authenticity from that source; but it has
also a further proof of a most interesting character,
derived from the existence of a copy in an Irish manu-

exclusively to Ireland until the twelfth century, when it also became
the name of the modern Scotland. It gradually ceased to be used of
Ireland. In the Epistles of St. Patrick, the Scoti are mentioned as then
the ruling race in Ireland.

[9] Preface to the Book of Hymns, part I, published by the Archæo-
logical and Celtic Society, Dublin, 1855; but Mr. Stokes thinks the
date should be the eleventh or twelfth century.

[1] Todd, p. 421.

[2] Trübner, 1872.

script[3] written between A.D. 680 and 691, and now preserved in the Ambrosian Library at Milan. This was originally in the library of Bobio in the Apennines, and has been twelve hundred years out of Ireland.

This Hymn was never placed within reach of the public until 1853,[4] when the Right Rev. Dr. Graves, Lord Bishop of Limerick, printed the translation which is now given here by his Lordship's kind permission, together with his illustrations from Holy Scripture.

The notes are for the most part taken from the ancient glosses or explanations in the Book of Hymns, which have been published since the Bishop's translation appeared. Those derived from this source are indicated by the letter G. The various readings which seemed to require notice have been added from the same source.

All the foregoing works have been lately published by Miss Cusack,[5] together with the Hymn of Fiacc, (eighth century,) and the Tripartite Life of St. Patrick; but notwithstanding the elaborate character of her book, it cannot be considered a satisfactory edition of his works. They are not supplied with the notes necessary for the elucidation of such ancient texts; the translation of the Irish Hymn is not taken from the best source, and that of the Hymn of Secundinus is really only a loose paraphrase, and therefore of scarcely any value. But the most serious blemish in her work is the placing the

[3] "The Antiphonary of Bangor" (in Ireland.) This work was first printed by Muratori. (A.D. 1713.) The Hymn had been previously printed from another source by Colgan in 1647, Sir J. Ware, 1656, and others.

[4] In the Catholic Layman, Dec., 1853.

[5] Life of St. Patrick. By M. F. Cusack. Longmans, 1871.

Tripartite Life in the same collection, and apparently on the same level as the genuine writings of St. Patrick, and dwelling so frequently on the pretended miracles. She complains that "they have scarcely been received with the credit they deserve even by Catholic writers;"[3] and again, "It is much to be feared that Catholics are by no means so firm in their faith on such subjects as they should be."[7]

Holding such strong opinions,[8] this lady is naturally in conflict with the best authorities on Irish Church history, not only, of course, with Dr. Todd, but with those of her own communion (the Roman Catholic.) Thus, Dr. O'Donovan, in his treatment of such matters, does not satisfy her; (page 552 of her work;) nor Dr. Lanigan, though a Roman Catholic clergyman; (364;) nor even Colgan, (358,) whose great fault is his credulity.

This treatment of the legendary element in the Tripartite and the introduction of an account of St. Patrick's Purgatory, a mediæval superstition which had nothing whatever to do with him, tend to confound truth and falsehood and mislead the enquirer.

The present work contains none but the original records of St. Patrick's mission, and is given to the

---

[6] Page 17.

[7] Page 24.

[8] Not satisfied with the prodigies of the Tripartite, Miss Cusack has culled from various sources a collection of marvels, which she presents to her readers, apparently with a view to facilitating the reception of those attributed to St. Patrick. There is, for instance, the young lady who "added a cubit to her stature," p. 307, note. The priest who was in two places at the same time, p. 258, note. The race-horses which were blessed by a saint, and thereby won a race ! p. 303, note.

public solely in the interests of truth; and not without the hope that some, finding, as they ascend to the source, how pure the doctrine is, may be led on farther still to the Holy Scriptures themselves, and "ask for the old paths where is the good way, and walk therein, and find rest for their souls."[9]

[9] Jeremiah vi. 16.

INTRODUCTION.

———◆———

1. THE sources from which the popular accounts of St. Patrick have been derived are the legendary Lives compiled during the middle ages by various authors known and unknown. These, as generally happens in such cases, become more minute in their details and more amazing in their prodigies the later their authors lived; and it is chiefly those of most modern date which afford the amplest materials for a sensational biography of him.

But though such a treatment of the subject may suit the popular taste, it does him serious injustice; for those who have taken the matter in hand, for the most part pass lightly over, or do not notice at all, those features of his character and missionary labours which are most worthy of record, and by the description they give us of him they repel the intelligent reader. For in the first place, they represent him as a worker of miracles, most of them of a childish and absurd[1] character. There may be some who believe them, or rather

---

[1] He lights a fire with icicles instead of sticks, (Jocelin, Life of St. Patrick, chap. v.) The water congeals in a kettle, notwithstanding the fire heaped around it (chap. xx.) A kid bleats from the stomach of a man who had stolen and eaten it, and afterwards returns to its owner uninjured, &c.

think they believe them, but the effect in most cases is to cause the rejection of his entire history; for as Dr. O'Donovan has observed, " The absurdity of the miracles attributed to St. Patrick by all his biographers, on every frivolous occasion, without number, measure, or use, has created a doubt in modern times of the truth of everything they relate."[2]

In the next place they misrepresent his mode of proceeding, from pure ignorance of what constitutes the character of a Christian missionary. Thus he curses rivers, territories, families, and individuals, for most trivial causes, and for the same reasons prophesies evil to people, though fortunately the fulfilment does not often follow.

The authors of these stories knew little of the spirit of our Lord's teaching, when he rebuked James and John for proposing to "command fire to come down from heaven and consume" the villagers who refused to receive Him: " Ye know not" (was His reply) " what manner of spirit ye are of, for the Son of man is not come to destroy men's lives, but to save them."[3] But these fable writers, when they represented St. Patrick as " flinging the bolt of his malediction,"[4] as they term it, on every trivial occasion, thought they were doing honour to his zeal and energy.

Again, to mention one more instance, they even make

[2] Annals of the Four Masters, A.D. 493, note.

[3] Luke ix. 54-56.

[4] It is painful to find a professing Christian in the nineteenth century approving of this. Yet Miss Cusack, referring to the story of his cursing a river at Wicklow, and thus depriving the fishermen of their livelihood says, " The miracle was undoubtedly one specially fitted to convert these rude and barbarous men," p. 226.

him dishonest. He steals; but this in their eyes is meritorious, as the plunder consists of relics which he filches from the sacred places at Rome for the benefit of Ireland. " O wondrous deed," exclaims the writer. " O rare theft of a vast treasure of holy things committed without sacrilege, the plunder of the most holy place in the world."[5]

In the present work the reader will find the true St. Patrick as he appears in his own Letters, his Hymn and his nephew's Poem. He will find there no miracles, no rendering of evil for evil, no pious thefts or frauds, but the language and acts of a single-minded, faithful, and devoted preacher of the Gospel of Christ.

It is remarkable that for many ages, and down to a late period, these authentic and most interesting remains were comparatively unknown. In the seventeenth century one of the most diligent students[6] of our ecclesiastical history never saw the Letters.

The Irish Hymn was unknown to all except the learned, until published by Dr. Petrie, and it is only twenty years since the Poem of Secundinus was translated for the first time. But perhaps the explanation may be that owing to their purity and simplicity, they were not so well suited to the public taste as the sensational stories which abound in the cheap popular Lives. Yet, whoever desires to know the truth about St. Patrick, and is willing to judge for himself, will find in them ample means of ascertaining it.

It is to be regretted that they afford but little information as to the history of his life, the writers confining

---

5 Vit. Tripart. iii. 82.   6 Colgan.

themselves to the spiritual aspect of the work and the principles on which it was conducted : a few notices in the early part of the *Confessio* are all that we find on the subject.

Whatever facts have come down to us are scattered through the legendary Lives, and to disentangle them is one of the objects of the learned work of Dr. Todd. Even he, however, with all his patience and critical skill, has sometimes failed to arrive at a certain conclusion, and many important portions of St. Patrick's life are still involved in obscurity. But enough may be considered as established to afford materials for an outline of his labours, which, while not pretending to the title of a biography, may be acceptable as sketches of missionary life in Ireland in the fifth century.

2. But here it should be mentioned that St. Patrick was not the first missionary to Ireland of whom we have an account.   That title belongs to Palladius, who was sent A.D. 431,[7] "to the Scoti [Irish] believing in Christ," by Celestine, who, as Bishop of the greatest city in the world, the centre of ancient civilization and learning, used his position in this instance for the furtherance of religion.   In modern times a similar course has been pursued by the Archbishops of Canterbury, in sending forth Bishops and Clergy to territories outside the British Empire, which have no claim on them beyond the general obligation " to sow beside all waters" the seed of the Gospel of Christ.

In the present instance Celestine seems to have been ill-informed ; for though there were some Christians, and

_____
[7] The Chronicle of Prosper.

perhaps a few congregations, scattered through the country, the Irish tribes were still Pagans, and exhibited violent hostility to Palladius' mission.

At Rome, Celestine was fondly believed to have "made the barbarous[8] island Christian;" but native Irish authority informs us on the contrary that his missionary failed signally. " God hindered him," (says a very ancient writer,) " for no man can receive anything from earth, unless it be given him from Heaven ; for neither did those fierce and savage men receive his doctrine readily, nor did he himself wish to spend time in a land not his own, but he returned to him that sent him."[9]

The hostile reception he met with, stands in singular contrast with that afterwards given to St. Patrick; and it is possible that some light may be thrown on it by the circumstance of his having a mission from Rome. Ages of warfare between the Irish clansmen and the Roman troops in North Britain[1] and elsewhere, had created hostile feelings ; and at one time the Romans went so far as to plan the conquest of Ireland—believing that " it would be an advantage to them in their contest with Britain, if the Roman arms should appear everywhere triumphant, and liberty entirely removed

---

[8] *Barbarous* (Prosper, Contra Collatorem.) The name was accepted by the Irish with the meaning of non-Roman (p.— note.) Ireland was outside the Roman Empire, and spoke a different language—a fact which is the key to many peculiarities in her subsequent history.

[9] Muircu Maccu Machtheni, in the Book of Armagh.

[1] The Irish King, Niall of the Nine Hostages, who died A.D. 405, made incursions into Britain against Stilicho. The Poet Claudian describes the sea as " foaming with his hostile oars."—See O'Donovan, Annals of Four Masters, A.D. 405.

out of sight,"[2] but the design was never carried out. A rivalry between the island in the far west and the world-wide empire, may excite a smile, but the Irish looking at it from their own insular point of view, were by no means disposed to admit their inferiority.[3]

Now, if Palladius' mission had a distinctly Roman character, as we may perhaps infer from his naming one of the churches he founded " the House [Church] of the Romans," and if there was in his demeanour any tincture of that pride by which Augustine at a later period offended the Britons, we cannot be greatly surprised at the abortive result of his mission. But whatever the cause, or combination of causes, which led to the result, he abandoned the mission after a very brief trial, and left the work to be taken up by one, who by common consent is termed the Apostle of Ireland.

3. Whether the date of St. Patrick's arrival was A.D. 432, as has been generally believed, or A.D. 442, as has been recently maintained[4] with much learning by Rev. Dr. Todd, it is not necessary to the purpose of the present work to inquire, nor perhaps are materials available as yet for a final decision.

The account of his early life in the *Confessio* is very brief. He tells us that at sixteen years of age he was living at a place called Bannaven Taberniæ, which is generally identified with Alcluaid, now Dumbarton, in

---

[2] Tacitus, vita Agricolæ.

[3] The Irish had their books of Synchronisms, in which were "marked what kings of the Assyrians, Medes, Persians, Greeks, and what *Emperors of the Romans*, were contemporary with the several monarchs of Erin in succession."—O'Curry, Lectures, p. 521.

[4] Todd, St. Patrick, p. 391-398.

Scotland. This city was the western post of the wall or entrenchment originally thrown up by Agricola, between the Clyde and the Forth, as a barrier against the incursions of the Picts and Scots. A border fortress occupied by Roman troops, ever on the alert to repel the inroads of an active enemy, was a most unfavourable position for the growth of youthful piety, or the diligent cultivation of knowledge, and it is no matter of surprise when he gives us to understand that his deficiencies were great in both respects.[5]

He belonged to what may be termed a clerical family, three generations of which had been in holy orders. His pedigree is thus given in the Confessio.

Odissus[6]	... ...	a Deacon.
|		
Potitus	... ...	a Priest.
|		
Calpornius	... ...	a Deacon.
|		
Sucat or Patricius	...	Apostle of Ireland.

[5] Confessio, chap. i, sec. 1, 3, 4, and chap. iii. sec. 12.

[6] In the Book of Rights St. Patrick is termed " the descendant of the Deacon." On this Dr. O'Donovan says in a note, " *recte*, son of the Deacon, i.e. Calpornius," but he evidently overlooked the following passage in the Hymn of Fiacc.

> Mac Calpurn, Maic Otide,
> Hoa Deochain Odisse.

> " Son of Calpurn, Son of Potitus,
> Grandson of Deacon Odisse."

It was scarcely worth while for Miss Cusack (p. 559) to disguise this latter fact, by leaving the Irish word for Deacon *untranslated*. In her work the line is

> Grandson of *Deochain Odissus*,

which the non-Celtic reader will naturally take for a proper name.

The descent from Odissus is noticed in the Armagh copy of the Confessio.

These facts are interesting, as reminding us that in early times marriage was reckoned "honourable in all,"[7] clergy as well as laity, as it is in the churches of England and Ireland, as well as in the Eastern Church at the present day.

The view of St. Patrick on this subject may be gathered from a passage in the annotations Tirechan, where he inquires of one of his disciples " the materials of a bishop from his disciples in Leinster," (i.e., a suitable person to consecrate as bishop,) and mentions that he must be a man, " free, of good family, without disgrace, without blemish, whose wealth is not too little, is not too great. I wish a *man of one wife* to whom hath not been born save one child."[8]

But we probably owe his mention of his clerical descent to his desire to prove that he was freeborn; for having been at first a slave in Ireland, as we shall presently see, it was important to make it clear that this was not his original condition. The " Scotic Princes" of whom he speaks, would have disdained to accept the teaching of a slave. This was also perhaps his reason for assuming the name of Patricius,[9] by which he is known as a missionary in Ireland.

[7] Heb. xiii. 4.

[8] Book of Armagh, A.D. 807, Goidelica, p. 91. (See 1 Tim. iii. 2.)

[9] See Confess. sec. 1, note. The title of Patrician was first borne by the descendants of the Roman senators of the time of Romulus. In later times it became merely a personal title. Agricola, whose intended invasion of Ireland has been referred to, was created Patricius by Vespasian. (Gibbon, ch. xvii. note.)

The higher the position St. Patrick occupied in his own country, the greater the sacrifice would be which he made in devoting himself to Ireland. He " sold his nobility for the good of others." (Ep. to Corot.

He had received at his baptism the name of Sucat,[1] but it seems to have been a custom with those who lived on the frontiers of the empire to drop the names given to them in their native dialects, and to adopt others more suited to civilized ears. At home the title of Patricius had long lost its peculiar meaning, but among the far-off Celtic tribes of Ireland it was still invested with some of its original importance, and would no doubt impress the chieftains with a sense of his dignity.

This, however, is an anticipation, as many years were yet to pass before the thought of devoting himself to the conversion of the Irish took possession of his mind.

5. The reader will find in the Confessio the account of his capture in an Irish expedition, his six years of slavery in Ireland with Milchu, chieftain of North Dalaradia, near Slemish, in the county Antrim, and the great spiritual change which passed over him. "There (he says) the Lord brought me to a sense of my unbelief, that I might even at a late season call my sins to remembrance, and turn with all my heart to the Lord my God, who regarded my low estate, and taking pity on my youth and ignorance, guarded me before I knew him, or could understand anything, or distinguish between good and evil, and strengthened and comforted me, as a father does his son."

6. Escaping from Ireland, he returned to his parents,

---

i. sec. 5.) He gave up country and parents, and was ready to give his life also, (Ibid., sec. 1,) He feared even to leave Ireland for a time, to visit his relatives and friends, much as he wished it, lest his work should suffer.—(Confess. ch. iv. 19.)

[1] " Su-cat from *Su*, now *Hu*, Deus, and *cat*, bellum, i.e. God of war." Stokes, Goidelica, p. 128, second ed.

but he could not rest; the unhappy condition of the Irish Heathen, " worshipping idols and unclean things," recurred to his mind; he saw in a vision of the night a man whose name was Victoricus, coming as if from Ireland with innumerable letters, one of which he gave him beginning thus, " the voice of the Irish people ;"[2] at the same moment he seemed to hear voices from the West of Ireland entreating him to come and dwell among them. This determined his course, and thenceforward he looked on the work as appointed for him. The influence exercised on him by dreams, at critical periods of his life, is plain from his own words, yet no man was ever less of a visionary. Their effect was rather to awaken his memory to passages of Scripture,[3] which he had overlooked or forgotten, and thus indirectly to influence his actions. He assures us that he had "no occasion except the Gospel and its promises to return to Ireland ;" and those promises vividly impressed on his mind in the manner referred to, were to him a call which he could not resist, and thus :—

" The Lord chose him to teach the barbarous nations."[4]

He does not inform us where or by whom he was consecrated, but the earliest accounts state that it was in Gaul, and by a bishop named Amathorex ;[5] and this

---

[2] *Hiberionacum.* This is the word used to express the mass of the people, as distinct from the Scoti, who were the ruling class. It was the degraded state of the general population which had touched his heart.

[3] Confess. chap. iii. sec. 12.

[4] Secundinus, Stanza D.

[5] The Book of Armagh, quoted in Todd, p. 317. The connection of St. Patrick with Gaul is an unpleasant fact to some, and an effort has lately been made by Monsignore Moran to get rid of it in a way,

is the more probable from his intimate connection[6] with that country, from which, as we shall presently see, there can be no doubt that he derived his mission.

7. Starting on his voyage with several companions from Gaul, he coasted along the eastern shore of Ireland, often short of provisions, and suffering many hardships, until he reached Strangford Lough in the county of Down, where he landed, and began his work.

When Onesimus ran away[7] from his master, he became convinced that it was his duty to return to him again, in accordance with the precept of St. Paul, "Let every man abide in the same calling wherein he was called. Art thou called being a servant? care not for it; but if thou mayest be made free use it rather."[8]

In the spirit of Onesimus, St. Patrick's first thought was of the master whom he had wronged by fleeing from him. To return to captivity was impossible; but he would offer him instead a "double ransom; an earthly one—namely, in money and worldly goods, and a spiritual one, by making known to him the Christian faith, and the Gospel way of salvation."[9]

which, if not ingenious, is at any rate off-hand. Instead of Gaul, he says, the writer must have meant "Italy," and instead of Amathorex, he must have intended "Maximus of Turin." But in this way, to use the words of Bishop Butler, "anything may be made of anything." The assertion of Dr. Moran that "Maximus in the old Celtic form would be precisely Amator," is a little amazing. The name Amathorex is purely Gaulish, and the termination "rex or rix," frequent in such names, has puzzled the later biographers, who, thinking it meant king, as in Latin, translate the name, "Amatus the king." Sometimes again they shorten it to Amator. Todd, p. 317, note. Miss Cusack, Life of St. Patrick, p. 215-219.

[6] Confes. sec. 5, 6, 19.   [8] 1 Cor. vii. 20, 21.
[7] Epistle to Philemon.   [9] Todd, p. 404.

C

Proceeding to explore the country, he and his companions were mistaken for enemies, and narrowly escaped being slain ; but their peaceful aspect was recognized in good time by Dichu, prince of the territory, who received them hospitably, and became a believer, " the first of the Scoti [Irish]" who confessed the faith under St. Patrick's ministry.

From this place he set out on foot to the residence of his former master ; but his well meant efforts for his conversion were ineffectual, and he had to return without accomplishing his object.

8. Without attempting to follow his footsteps during his many years of labour in Ireland, we may now notice some striking passages which throw light on his work ; and first of his preaching at Tara. Having laid the foundation of Christianity in Ulster, he resolved to visit the residence of the Irish kings, and preach Christ in the very citadel of idolatry. Sailing southward, he entered the mouth of the river Boyne, and leaving his boats there, proceeded on foot to execute his mission. While on his way an interesting circumstance occurred, which brings out the gentleness of his character. The party had gone to the house of a respectable person, in one of those circular enclosures where the Irish chieftains at this time lived.[1] The family became believers ; and when they were retiring to rest, one of the children, a little boy, insisted on sleeping with St. Patrick, and in the morning when the saint was getting into his chariot, and had one foot in and the other on the ground, the child held his foot tightly with both hands, and cried,

---

[1] These are erroneously called Danish forts, they were really built by the ancient Irish, and are called in Irish, *Lios*, or *Rath*.

" Let me go with Patrick, my true father." He was allowed to go, and became his constant companion, and afterwards, under the name of Benignus, his successor at Armagh.[2]

Having reached the neighbourhood of Tara on the eve of Easter, he made preparations for celebrating the festival, and proceeded to light his paschal fire on the hill of Slane; but at this very time a great Pagan festival occurred, which began by the extinguishing of every fire in that country, and " whosoever kindled one before the king's fire appeared on the hill of Tara, that soul should be cut off from his people."

No sooner had the bright flame of the strange fire shot up into the evening air than the Druids recognised a rival power; they declared that "the fire should be immediately extinguished, else it would get the better of their fires, and bring about the downfall of the kingdom."

This was the first open contest between Christianity and Druidism in Ireland. It was a critical moment, and the fate of his mission hung in the balance; but he was strong in the Lord and the power of His might. " Some" (he is reported to have said) " put their trust in chariots, and some in horses, but we will remember the name of the Lord."[3]

Ordered to appear before the king, the opportunity was afforded him, which he so much desired, of preaching the Gospel in the presence of the rulers of the kingdom. It was on this occasion that he composed the " Irish Hymn," which he sang as he approached the

---

[2] Book of Armagh.   [3] Psalm xx. 7.

palace, and thus gave all present to understand the foundation on which his courage rested.

His exhortations failed to convince the king, though several of his followers became obedient to the faith; but he had gained much by successfully encountering the Druids in the headquarters of their system, and he was thenceforward assured of victory.

9. From this instance of moral courage and Christian faith we pass on to notice a proof of his readiness to " endure hardship as a good soldier of Jesus Christ."[4]

He had dreamed many years before that he heard the children at the wood of Foclud[5] calling him to come over and dwell with them; and now the time was come, when " the Lord would grant them according to their cry," and he prepared for the journey. It was a perilous one, for his path lay straight across the island to Killala, near the brink of the Atlantic; and the Ireland of the fifth century was very unlike this of the nineteenth. Primæval forests[6] clothed the hills, and stretched far over the plains; in his way lay morasses and dense jungles, afterwards called " fastnesses;" the rivers were unbridged; the wild boar and the wolf roamed through the land, and, fiercer still than these, the lawless inhabitants of those remote regions lay in wait ready to make him a prisoner, or to put him to death. The hardships

---

[4] 2 Tim. ii. 3.

[5] Confess. ch. iii. sec. 10. In the nineteenth as in the fifth century, it is the far West which calls most loudly for missionary labour.

[6] One of the earliest names of Ireland was *Inis na bhfiodhbhadh*, (veeva,) " the Island of the Woods." Even in the time of Giraldus Cambrensis, A.D. 1192, it was computed that the greater part of the country was clothed with forests.

he underwent in such journeys are alluded to in the following passage from the Hymn of Fiacc :—

" He slept on a bare stone ; and a wet robe around him.
A pillar stone was his pillow; he left not his body in warmth."[7]

His preparations for the journey show much forethought; for, though eminently a man of faith, he did not deem it his duty to run needless risks. He first engaged as an escort the sons of Amalgaid, (Awley,)[8] chief of the territory, thus securing the protection of that tribe. He further paid black-mail, (" the price of fifteen men,") to obtain protection from " bad men," probably marauders of other districts through which he passed. Arrived at his destination after many perils, the tribe assembled at their meeting place to receive him and hear his message, and there he preached the Gospel to them. It is to be regretted that no account of this or any of his discourses has been preserved ; but the author who describes the scene adds, " He penetrated the hearts of all, and led them to embrace cordially the Christian faith and doctrine."

10. In the absence of an account of any of his sermons, a dialogue is worthy of notice, which is said, on ancient authority, to have taken place between him and two daughters of the king of Ireland. The two young women had come out in the early morning to a well, hard by which they found St. Patrick and his party sitting.[9] With eager curiosity they accost the

---

[7] Goidelica, p. 131.

[8] From whom the barony derives the name of Tirawley, i.e., the land of Awley.

[9] This incident took place near Cruachan, now Rathcroghan in the county of Roscommon, an ancient residence of the kings of Connaught.

unknown strangers : " Where are ye ? and whence come ye ?" and then they press him with many questions :

Who is God ?

And where is God ?

And of what [nature] is God ?

And where is His dwelling-place ?

Has your God sons and daughters, gold and silver?

Is He everlasting ?

Is He beautiful ?

Did many foster His Son ?

Are His daughters dear and beauteous to men of the world ?

Is He in heaven or in earth?

In the sea ?

In rivers ?

In mountainous places ?

In valleys ?

Declare unto us the knowledge of Him ?

How shall He be seen ?

How is He to be loved ?

How is He to be found ?

Is it in youth ?

Is it in old age that He is to be found ?

The young women, astonished at the unusual aspect of the strangers, thought they must be "men fairies, or gods of the earth, or phantoms."

Colgan has the following note : " Imaginary spirits (*spiritus phantastici*) are called *viri sidhe*, (men of the hills) because they seem as if to come forth from pleasant hills to trouble mankind ; and because the vulgar think they live in subterranean dwellings within those hills. These dwellings, and sometimes the hills themselves, are called by the Irish *sidhe or siodha*." Vit. Tert. note 49 ; Trias Thaum. p. 32a. The female form of this compound, bean-sidhe (banshee) is familiar to most readers.

But St. Patrick, full of the Holy Ghost, answered and said—

Our God is the God of all men.

The God of heaven and earth, of the sea and rivers.

The God of the sun, the moon, and all stars.

The God of the high mountains, and of the lowly valleys.

The God who is above heaven, in heaven, and under heaven.

He hath a habitation in the heaven, and the earth, and the sea, and all that are therein.

He inspireth all things.

He quickeneth all things.

He is over all things.

He sustaineth all things.

He giveth light to the light of the sun.

He illuminates the night by his brightness.

And He hath made springs in a dry ground.

And dry islands in the sea.

And hath appointed the stars to serve the greater lights.

He hath a Son co-eternal and co-equal with Himself.

The Son is not younger than the Father.

Nor is the Father older than the Son.

And the Holy Ghost breatheth in them.

The Father and the Son and the Holy Ghost are not divided.

But I desire to unite you to the Heavenly King, inasmuch as you are the daughters of an earthly king.

And the virgins said, as with one mouth and one heart, "Teach us most diligently how we may believe in the Heavenly King. Show us how we may see Him face to face, and whatsoever thou shalt say unto us, we will do."

And accordingly, after further instruction in the doctrines of Baptism, Repentance, the Resurrection, Judgment to come, and the Unity of the Church, "they were baptized, and a white garment put upon their heads."[1]

This remarkable catechism, if it may be so called, bears evidence of high authority, and probably preserves some of St. Patrick's teaching. We may infer from it the care with which he instructed those who desired to become Christians.

In such labours as these he was engaged during many following years, until A.D. 457, when we find him founding the ecclesiastical establishment at Armagh, which has since occupied the foremost place in the Irish Church.

The site was a gift from Dairi, chief of the territory, and the manner of its bestowal is told in an interesting way in the Book of Armagh.

The story contains some marvellous incidents, as we might expect from a work compiled eleven hundred years ago ; but making a little allowance for the writer's fancy, it has evidently a groundwork of truth, and for this reason, and because it gives us a life-like picture of his

[1] Todd, 452-455. There is an absurd story of St. Patrick when baptising Aengus, king of Cashel, having inadvertently pierced his foot with his crozier, and only discovered it when the ceremony was over. He then asked the king why he had not told him? who replied that he thought it was part of the usual ceremony! The story which is told as honourable to the king, would really be only a proof of his ignorance, if it were true, which it is not.—Todd. 468.

dealings with the Irish chieftains, it seems worth while to give it here.

11. "There lived in the territory of the Easterns a man both rich and honourable, whose name was Dairi, and Patrick asked of him to grant a place for the exercise of his religion. And the rich man said to the saint, 'What place dost thou desire?' 'I pray of thee [said Patrick] to bestow upon me that eminence which is called the *Sallow Ridge*, and there I will build me a place.' Notwithstanding, he would not grant to the saint that high ground, but he gave him another portion in a lower situation, where is now the *Fertæ Martyrum*, beside Armagh, and there Patrick abode with his disciples."

Then follows an account of a trespass committed on the ground thus bestowed, in consequence of which Dairi's horse is struck dead.

The chieftain orders Patrick to be slain, but is himself seized by sudden illness; Patrick then cures him, and restores the horse to life. After this little embellishment of the narrative it proceeds—"After this Dairi came that he might do honour to the saint, and brought with him a valuable imported caldron, which held three firkins. And Dairi said to the saint, 'Thou mayest have this caldron.' And Patrick said, '*Grazacham*.'[2] Then Dairi returned home and said, 'The man is a fool who hath not a civil word to say but *Grazacham* in return for the beautiful three-firkin caldron.' Moreover, Dairi said to his servants, 'Go and bring me back my

---

[2] *Grazacham*, an abbreviation of the Latin phrase *Gratias-agam*—I give thanks. The Celtic chieftain did not understand the Latin, belonging as he did to a people who were "foreign to the Roman language."

caldron.' So they came and said to Patrick, 'We must take away the caldron.' Notwithstanding, on this occasion also, Patrick said, *Grazacham*, you may take it away. So they took it away. And Dairi inquired of his servants what the Christian said when they took back the caldron, and they replied, ' He said *Grazacham*.' Then Dairi answered and said, ' *Grazacham* when we give, and *Grazacham* when we take away, surely this *Grazacham* of his must be a good word; therefore the brazen caldron shall be restored to him.' And this time Dairi came in person carrying the caldron to St. Patrick, and said to him, ' Thy caldron shall remain with thee, for thou art an upright and unswerving man. Moreover, I now grant to thee my whole right in that portion of ground, which thou formerly didst desire, and dwell thou there.' And that is the city that is now called Armagh.

"And they went forth together, both St. Patrick and Dairi, to view the admirable and well-pleasing gift, and they ascended the height, and found a roe and a little fawn with her, lying on the spot where the altar of the Northern Church of Armagh now stands. And St. Patrick's companions wanted to catch the fawn and kill it ; but the saint objected, and would not permit them ; nay, he even took up the fawn himself, and carried it on his shoulders, and the roe followed him like a pet sheep, until he laid down the fawn on another eminence at the north side of Armagh."[3]

The former story brings to mind the words of St. Paul: "I know both how to be abased and I know how to abound:

[3] The Ancient Churches of Armagh, by Rev. Wm. Reeves, D.D. p. 6.

everywhere and in all things I am instructed both to be full and to be hungry, both to abound and to suffer need;" a passage which seems to have been often in his thoughts.[4]

12. His biographers relate that in the later years of his life he called together Assemblies or Synods, to complete the organization of the Church. The proceedings of the Synods or Synod held at this period would be of interest if they had come down to us uncorrupted; but it is unfortunate that the canons which are now in existence, purporting to be the result of their deliberations, are so interpolated and altered as to be of no value as evidence.

Thus, in the sixth canon of the Synod known as that of "Patrick, Auxilius, and Iserninus,"[5] "the Roman tonsure" is directed to be practised; whereas, it was not until A.D. 718, or more than two hundred years after St. Patrick's time, that this innovation was adopted at Hy or Iona, the famous seat of Irish learning. It is clearly impossible, therefore, that St. Patrick could have been the author of this canon.[6]

This and other reasons go to prove that these canons, so far from belonging to the age of St. Patrick, are

[4] Phil, iv. 12. Conf. iii. 14.

[5] Villanueva, Can. vi.

[6] The disputes about the Irish and Roman tonsures, which seem so trivial to us, perhaps owed their violence to the strong National feeling of the Irish. The former, which was introduced by St. Patrick, (probably from Gaul—Lanigan, iii. 72,) consisted in shaving all the hair in front of a line drawn over the top of the head, from ear to ear. This was the *National* custom. ("Ex consuetudine Patria." Bede, lib. v. cap. 21.) The Roman tonsure consisted in shaving a circle on the top of the head.—Todd, 487.

really in their present shape as late as the ninth or tenth century,[7] and therefore cannot be relied on as evidence of his opinions.

Yet, the late professor of Irish History in the "Catholic University" treats them as genuine, without the faintest hint of their interpolation. Thus he tells the students of that institution that one of these canons "affords a proof so unanswerable as to dispose for ever of the modern imposition so pertinaciously practised upon a large section of our countrymen, as well as upon foreigners speaking the English language; namely, that the primitive Church of Ireland did not acknowledge or submit to the Pope's supremacy, or appeal to it in cases of ecclesiastical necessity and difficulty."[8]

It may have been, however, that he was not aware of the facts which Dr. Todd has pointed out.

13. The life of the great missionary was now drawing to a close. The scene of his early missionary labours was Saul, near Downpatrick, and there it was appointed that they should conclude.

Feeling that his last illness was approaching, he wished to hasten to Armagh to breathe his last sigh in his favourite spot; but becoming rapidly worse, he was brought back to Saul, and there passed to his rest, A.D. 493, leaving a name which, as his genuine works become known, will grow in the affections of those who admire a great and faithful preacher of the Gospel of Christ.

The picture of his success is sometimes drawn in very brilliant colours; it is said to have been rapid, bloodless, and complete; but this description is far from accurate.

[7] Todd, p. 488.
[8] O'Curry's Lectures, 1861, p. 373.

Missionary life has its successes and failures, its joys and sorrows; and if we are told of a career all sunshine and no shadow, we instinctively feel that the picture is overdrawn.

His mission was no exception to this rule. He met with frequent opposition; his life was threatened and plotted against; on one occasion his charioteer was killed in mistake for himself; many rejected his authority, and it has been inferred (according to Dr. Todd) from his placing fortifications around his ecclesiastical establishments that he had little confidence in their security. Yet, after making all the allowance that truth requires, a survey of his labours will convince us that he occupies one of the very highest positions among the soldiers of the cross, and is justly entitled to the honour of being named the " Apostle of Ireland."

His success was due to the causes which at all times sway the minds and hearts of men. Unwearied in labour, his zeal never cooled from the moment he landed in Ireland till the end came. His courage and firmness were tried in many a danger, and gained the respect of the fiery and impulsive chieftains; and yet he was also gentle of disposition,[9] and gifted with such a charm of manner as quickly won the affections of the young. Devoid of learning, owing to the calamity which befel him in youth, his wisdom more than compensated for the deficiency. It is at all times conspicuous, and in no instance more than in his addressing himself, first of all, to the chieftains, before seeking to gain over the

[9] See the incident of the fawn, p. 26, and the story of Benignus, p. 18.

tribes which they ruled. Above all, he used the divinely appointed means of winning souls to Christ. He was—

" A true and excellent cultivator of the Gospel field,
  Whose seeds are seen to be the Gospels of Christ,
  Which he sows from his divine mouth in the ears of the wise,
  And tills their hearts and minds with the Holy Spirit." [1]

14. Before proceeding to notice the works which follow, it is desirable to offer some observations here on the source of his mission and the nature of his teachings—subjects on which, as is well-known, there has been much controversy: some maintaining that he was sent from Rome, and taught Roman doctrine, as understood at the present day; others that he had no connection with the Roman Church, and held no doctrine but what may be read in Holy Scripture or proved thereby. On one side is an inert mass of popular prejudice and traditional belief, while on the other are reason and evidence, which must eventually make their way in spite of all opposition. Did he then come from Rome?

The first reply to this question is, that his own works are totally silent on the subject. He never mentions the Pope or the Roman See. Neither does Secundinus. Is it credible that if he was a Roman missionary he should never allude to the fact in any way directly or indirectly? Can any one imagine a Papal legate of the present day never once, in pastoral or public address, mentioning the Pope, or his nephew maintaining a similar reserve?

To the silence of the documents in the present work must be added that of Prosper, the Roman chronicler,

[1] Secundinus, stanza v.

(A.D. 463,) who makes so much of the sending of Palladius; and also of the Hymn of Fiacc, which is probably as late as the eighth century.

If this uniform silence of the earliest writings is not sufficient to convince, we may further appeal to the language of certain distinguished Irishmen who laboured among the Anglo Saxons about a century and a-half after his time. A dispute having arisen between them and the Roman clergy who were engaged in the same work in Britain, a Synod was held at Whitby, in Yorkshire, to decide the question, which had reference to the different modes of observing Easter practised in the Irish and Roman Churches. On this occasion the Roman clergy gave as the authority for their usage, "Peter the blessed Prince of the Apostles," while the Irish said they followed "the blessed Evangelist St. John, the disciple specially beloved by our Lord, and all the Churches over which he presided:"[2] in other words, they followed the Eastern Church. Now this would be incomprehensible if St. Patrick, the founder of the Irish Church, had come from Rome and brought the Roman customs with him.

The history of the Church at home is also against the Roman mission; for "if [says Dr. Neander] St. Patrick came as a deputy to Ireland from Rome, it might naturally be expected that in the Irish Church a certain sense of dependence would always have been preserved towards the mother Church at Rome. But we find, on the contrary, in the Irish Church afterwards a spirit of Church freedom similar to that shown by the

---

[2] Bede, Lib. III. Cap. xxv.

ancient British Church, which struggled against the yoke of Roman ordinances.[3]"

For these reasons the story of his mission from Rome may be set aside as altogether opposed to evidence.[4]

15. But then from what Church did he come? Appealing again to his own works, we find him several times referring to Gaul, (France,) and mentioning "his brethren" there, whom he also calls "the Lord's saints,"[5] in terms of affection. These were evidently the Gallican clergy. He makes no mention of any others. Further, there is very ancient though not contemporary authority, as has already been mentioned, for his ordination in Gaul by a bishop named Amathorex; and the introduction by him into Ireland of a peculiar tonsure, supposed to be derived from the Church of Gaul, is in harmony with this statement.

We may therefore, with the utmost probability, assume that he belonged to the Church of Gaul, and this

---

[3] Hist. Chris. Relig. and Ch., p. 174.

[4] Notwithstanding these facts, Cardinal Cullen uses the following language in his Pastoral, issued in the spring of 1872:—"The most ancient writers of his life attest that he would not commence his sacred work till he had received authority from St. Peter, whom he revered as the supreme head of the Church of Christ, and the source of all spiritual power; and they record the beautiful prayer which he poured forth when summoned by the angel Victor to the holy enterprise—'O Lord Jesus Christ, lead me, I beseech Thee, to the seat of the Holy Roman Church, that, receiving there authority to preach with confidence thy sacred truths, the Irish nation may through my ministry be gathered to the fold of Christ.'" Dr. Lanigan, however, who is a higher authority on Irish Ecclesiastical history, says there is no truth in these conversations with the angel Victor, (Eccl. His. I., 144, 145,) and we have seen above that the "most ancient writers," i.e., St. Patrick himself, and Secundinus, do not support the Cardinal's statement.

[5] Confess, secs. 5, 6, 19.

conclusion amounts to certainty, when we find that it is
the key to the understanding of the reference to the
Eastern Church made at the Synod of Whitby. There
was no direct communication with the East, and no
conceivable way in which the Irish could have learned
the Eastern practices, except through some other church,
which thus became a connecting link between the East
and West. This was exactly the position of Gaul. Its
southern coast had been colonized by Greeks before the
Christian era, and their connection with the East continued down to early Christian times. Several of the
bishops who occupied sees there were Asiatics, and one
of them, Irenæus, (A.D. 177-202,) took part in the controversy about Easter, between Polycrates, Bishop of
Ephesus and Pope Victor, and maintained the views of
the Eastern Church.

It is plain, therefore, that the influence of that church
was very powerful in the south of Gaul. Moreover, off
the coast (near Cannes) lies the island of St. Honorat,
formerly called Lerins, in which was a famous monastic
school, where, according to many of his biographers,[6] St.

---

[6] Lanigan, Vol. I., p. 174, chap. iv. sec. 12. This school is now chiefly
remembered through Vincentius of Lerins, the author of the well-
known test of Catholic truth—'' What has been believed always, everywhere, and by all, that is truly and properly Catholic,'' (*quod semper,
quod ubique, quod ab omnibus creditum est, hoc est vere proprieque
Catholicum.*) This has been often quoted as opposed to the Ro man
additions made to the primitive faith ; and recently at the Bonn Con-
ference, in August 1875, it was accepted by the Old Catholics as one
of the tests by which dogmas may be recognised, which, '' as regards
their origin and contents have their root in Divine Revelation.''

Vincentius flourished A.D. 434, and if we adopt the later date of St.
Patrick's mission, they might have been fellow-students.—See Hymn
of Secundinus, stanza R, note.

D

Patrick received his training for the mission on which his heart was set.

If this was so, there is no longer any difficulty in understanding how the Church of Ireland came to follow the Churches of the East in those usages in which they differed from Rome, and we see also, perhaps, why the Apocalypse[7] was his peculiar study ; as the last work of the Apostle, apart from other reasons, it would naturally be held in high regard by the Churches which followed his teaching.

Yet, though deriving his orders from the Church of Gaul, and associated with its clergy by ties of friendship, he ever regarded himself, not as commissioned by

---

[7] Secundinus says, Stanza Y :—

" He sings Hymns with the Apocalypse and the Psalms of God, on which also he discourses for the edification of the people of God." The peculiar regard in which the number seven was held in Ireland, of which the so-called Seven Churches are a well-known instance, has often been noticed. It may be that in the reference here we have a hint of its origin, for " the most careless reader of the Apocalypse must be struck with the manner in which almost everything there is ordered by sevens," (Trench, p. 59,) and accordingly we have in the Confessio, apparently, Seven Dreams, (secs. 6, 9, 9, 10, 11, 11, 12.) In the Irish Hymn we find (verse 2) seven facts in the life of Christ, and in verse 6, seven perils by which he was endangered. In making use of the Apocalypse, the Epistles to the Seven Churches would be sure to occupy much of his attention ; for, again to quote Archbishop Trench, " The practical interest of these Epistles in their bearing on the whole pastoral and ministerial work is extreme." The groups of Seven Churches in Ireland would seem to be an attempt to reproduce the Apocalyptic seven. In its remote origin this idea was Jewish. Thus Optatus of Milevi, A.D. 368, refers to seven synagogues on Mount Zion, " In illo Monte Sion in cujus vertice est non magna planities, in qua fuerant septem synagogæ ubi Judæorum populus conveniens, legem per Moysem datam discere potuisset."—Lib. iii. p. 62, Paris, 1631.

any human authority, but as directly summoned to the work by God. He tells us himself, his only motives were "the Gospel and its promises," and Secundinus adds, "He received his Apostleship from God," and this is further explained, "he was sent by God as an Apostle, even as Paul." Now St. Paul's description of himself is, that he was "an Apostle, not of men, neither by man, but by Jesus Christ, and God the Father, who raised him from the dead."[8]

Such was the view St. Patrick took of his mission to Ireland; and one whose labours tended so visibly to the promotion of God's glory might well regard himself as divinely guided in undertaking the work.

16. The question which has just occupied our attention is not so important as that which we have now to consider—namely, did St. Patrick teach what is now known as Roman Catholic doctrine, or if not, what else? Now there is no difficulty in answering this question, for at the commencement of his Confessio, he gives a Creed or summary of his faith; and if this is compared with that of Pope Pius IV., it will be seen at a glance whether they correspond or not. The latter, it will be observed, consists of two parts, the first being the ancient Creed of Nice and Constantinople, called the Nicene Creed, the second, consisting of the twelve new articles which form the addition afterwards made by the Church of Rome to the primitive faith.[9]

---

[8] Galatians i. 1.

[9] This creed was put forth A.D. 1564, and is now imposed on all Roman Catholic ecclesiastics.—See the Bishop of Lincoln on the Irish Church, No. xxvi. of his Occasional Sermons, sec. viii. note—a work in which the learned Prelate has done good service to the Irish Church.

ST. PATRICK'S CREED.

THERE is no other God, nor ever was, nor will be hereafter, except God the Father, unbegotten, without beginning; from whom is all beginning; who upholds all things.

And His Son, Jesus Christ, whom we acknowledge to have been always with the Father: who, before the beginning of the world, was spiritually present with the Father: begotten in an unspeakable manner before all beginning: by whom were made all things, visible and invisible: who was made man, and, having overcome death, was received into heaven to the Father: and He hath given Him a name which is above every name; that at the name of Jesus every knee should bow, of things in heaven, and things in earth, and things under the earth; and that every tongue should confess that Jesus Christ is Lord and God. In whom we believe; and we await His coming, who ere long shall judge the quick and dead. Who will render to every man according to his deeds.

And has poured out abundantly on us the gift of the Holy Spirit, even the earnest of immortality; who makes those that believe and obey to be the sons of God the Father and joint heirs with Christ. Whom we confess and adore, one God in the Trinity of the Sacred Name.

POPE PIUS IV.'s CREED.

I believe in one God, the Father Almighty, Maker of heaven and earth, and of all things visible and invisible.

And in one Lord Jesus Christ, the only begotten Son of God; begotten of His Father before all worlds. God of God, Light of Light, very God of very God; begotten, not made, being of one substance with the Father, by whom all things were made; who for us men and for our salvation came down from heaven, and was incarnate by the Holy Ghost of the Virgin Mary, and was made man; and was crucified also for us under Pontius Pilate. He suffered, and was buried; and the third day He rose again, according to the Scriptures; and ascended into heaven; and sitteth on the right hand of the Father. And He shall come again with glory to judge both the quick and the dead: whose kingdom shall have no end.

And I believe in the Holy Ghost, the Lord and Giver of Life, who proceedeth from the Father and the Son; who with the Father and the Son together is worshipped and glorified; who spake by the Prophets. And I believe one Catholic and Apostolic Church. I acknowledge one Baptism for the remission of sins; and I look for the resurrection of the dead; and the life of the world to come.

I. I most firmly admit and embrace Apostolical and Ecclesiastical traditions, and all other constitutions and observances of the same Church.

II. I also admit the sacred Scriptures, according to the sense which the Holy Mother Church has held and does hold, to whom it belongs to judge of the true sense and interpretation of the Holy Scriptures ; nor will I ever take or interpret them otherwise than according to the unanimous consent of the Fathers.

III. I profess, also, that there are truly and properly seven Sacraments of the new law, instituted by Jesus Christ our Lord, and for the salvation of mankind, though all are not necessary for every one : namely, Baptism, Confirmation, Eucharist, Penance, Extreme Unction, Orders, and Matrimony, and that they confer grace ; and of these, Baptism, Confirmation, and Orders cannot be reiterated without sacrilege. I also receive and admit the ceremonies of the Catholic Church, received and approved in the solemn administration of all the above said Sacraments.

IV. I receive and embrace all and every one of the things, which have been defined and declared in the Holy Council of Trent, concerning original sin and justification.

V. I profess, likewise, that in the Mass is offered to God a true, proper, and propitiatory sacrifice for the living and the dead ; and that in the most holy sacrifice of the Eucharist, there is truly, really, and substantially, the body and blood, together with the soul and divinity, of our Lord Jesus Christ ; and that there is made a conversion of the whole substance of the bread into the body, and of the whole substance of the wine into the blood, which conversion the Catholic Church calls transubstantiation. I confess, also, that under either kind alone, whole and entire, Christ and a true Sacrament are received.

VI. I constantly hold that there

is a purgatory, and that the souls detained therein are helped by the suffrages of the faithful.

VII. Likewise, that the saints, reigning together with Christ, are to be honoured and invocated; that they offer prayers to God for us ; and that their relics are to be venerated.

VIII. I most firmly assert that the images of Christ and of the Mother of God, ever Virgin, and also of the other saints, are to be had and retained, and that due honour and veneration are to be given them.

IX. I also affirm that the power of indulgences was left by Christ in the Church, and that the use of them is most wholesome to Christian people.

X. I acknowledge the Holy Catholic and Apostolical Roman Church, the mother and mistress of all Churches ; and I promise and swear true obedience to the Bishop of Rome, the successor of St. Peter the Prince of the Apostles, and Vicar of Jesus Christ.

XI. I also profess and undoubtedly receive all other things delivered, defined, and declared, by the sacred canons and general councils, and particularly by the Holy Council of Trent; and, likewise, I also condemn, reject, and anathematize, all things contrary thereto, and all heresies whatsoever condemned, rejected, and anathematized, by the Church.

XII. This true Catholic faith, out of which none can be saved, which I now freely profess and truly hold, I, N., promise, vow, and swear, most constantly to hold and profess the same, whole and entire, with God's assistance, to the end of my life.[1]

---

[1] This translation of the twelve new Articles is taken from Butler's Book of the Roman Catholic Church.

17. From this comparison, it is obvious that St. Patrick knew nothing of the twelve new Articles added to the primitive faith by the Church of Rome, nor will any trace of them be found in any part of the writings of himself or his nephew. He cannot therefore with any propriety be termed a *Roman* Catholic.[2]

On the other hand, we have the testimony of Secundinus that he was "a faithful witness of God in the CATHOLIC doctrine," that is, the doctrine held by the Universal[3] Church, or, as it is expressed by Vincentius of Lerins, "What has been believed everywhere, always, and by all." His position was therefore that of the Church of Ireland at the present day, as will more plainly appear from the following considerations :—

(1.) The faith she holds is stated in the Apostles', the Nicene, and the Athanasian Creeds, which are universally received, and may be proved by most certain warrant of Holy Scripture. Now it is plain from the comparison already instituted between his creed and

---

[2] Miss Cusack, it is true, finds in the Hymn of Secundinus (stanza C) evidence that St. Patrick taught "the unchangeable faith of the One Holy Catholic Apostolic Church of Rome." But on comparing her translation with the original, as given in her work, it will be seen that she is entirely wrong.

Constans in Dei timore	Constant in the service of God,
Et fide immobilis,	and immovable in the faith *of Peter*,
Super quem ædificatur,	upon whom the Church is built,
Ut Petrum, ecclesia,	and whose apostolate he received
Cujusque apostolatum	from God, *against whose gates the*
A Deo sortitus est,	*assaults of hell cannot prevail.*—p.
In cujus portæ adversus	514.
Inferni non prævalent. p. 563.	

In fact, the passage when correctly translated, (see p. 55 of the present work,) really bears strongly the opposite way.

[3] See Hymn of Secundinus, stanza Testis, note [2].

that of Nicea, that all he held she holds, and nothing
that she rejects was received by him.   There is therefore a substantial identity of doctrine between the
Church as founded by him in the fifth century and as
now existing in the nineteenth.

(2.) It is a cardinal principle of the Church of Ireland
that "Holy Scripture containeth all things necessary
to salvation."   Therefore, she directs it to be read in
such a language as the people may understand, and
promotes its free circulation, and urges upon all the
duty to read, mark, learn, and inwardly digest it.   Now
the practice of St. Patrick was in accordance with this
principle.   His Epistles abound in quotations from the
Bible, and where he does not directly refer to it, his
language bears the impress of its constant study.   No
one can read his writings without feeling the truth of
Tillemont's remark, "Surely he was well acquainted
with Holy Scripture."

This is further evident from the account of his
preaching given by Secundinus.

"He finds in the Sacred Volume a Sacred Treasure." *stanza* Sacrum.
"His words are seasoned with the Divine oracles."   ,,   Testis.
"His seeds are seen to be the Gospels of Christ."   ,,   Uerus.
"He sings Hymns, with the Apocalypse, and
   The Psalms of God, on which also he discourses
   For the edification of the people of God."   ,,   Ymnos.

This character of his teaching is well illustrated by
the epistle to Coroticus : when he has occasion to rebuke
that cruel chieftain, instead of pronouncing anathemas
against him in the manner of the legendary Lives, he
quotes the threatenings of Holy Scripture, and by the
"terrors of the Lord," seeks to alarm and persuade ;
and again, when it is needful to speak words of cheer to

his persecuted people, he uses the eloquent promises of the Apocalypse[4] to comfort them ; and thus the Scripture was in his hands, "profitable for doctrine, for reproof, for correction, for instruction in righteousness."

We might naturally infer that the Bible, which was the subject of his preaching, was also the companion of his private hours ; but we are not left to conjecture, as we have positive proof on the point ; for at the Royal Irish Academy in Dublin may be seen a manuscript of the Gospels, generally believed to be the copy which he brought with him to Ireland. This interesting relic is contained in a case of yew, which was again enclosed in a silver casket[5] by the veneration of a later age. Few objects should have a deeper interest for Irishmen than this memorial of his missionary labours. Not only, however, did he possess it for himself, but he desired that others should have it. He circulated the Bible. Thus, we read in the Book of Armagh : "He took with him the books of the Law and the books of the Gospel (the Old and New Testaments) and left them in new places."[6] This primitive custom of placing a copy of the Holy Scriptures in every church was revived at the Reformation. Thus, in the reign of Elizabeth, "a large Bible . . . . . was placed in the middle of

---

[4] "Oftentimes (says Archbishop Trench) slighted by the Church in times of prosperity, it is made much of, and its preciousness, as it were instinctively discovered, in times of adversity and fiery trial." (Seven Churches, p. 22.)

[5] The Domhnach Airgid. (See Trans. of Royal Irish Academy, vol. xviii., Antiq. p. 14, and O'Curry's Lectures, p. 322.

[6] Portavit Patricius per Sininn secum . . . . libros legis, evangelii libros, et reliquit illos in locis novis.—Betham, Irish Antiquarian Researches, App. p. 17.

the choir of each cathedral. of Christ's Church, and St. Patrick's, (in Dublin,) where on their being first offered to public view they caused a great resort of the people thither to read and hear their contents."[7] Sometimes we even find him writing out a copy of the Psalms, himself, for a youthful convert.

The example of its founder gave a tone to the Irish Church, which it long retained. It became a Church famous for the study and interpretation of Holy Scripture; and before a century had elapsed, its high reputation attracted students from all quarters to the shores of Ireland.

(3.) Turning next to the constitution of the Church, we find no mention of any ecclesiastical rank, or any orders of the ministry, but those of bishops, priests, and deacons. The absence of all allusion to the Pope has been already adverted to, and the inference from this plainly is, that the Church, perfectly constituted according to the Apostolic model, with the threefold order of the ministry, needed not, and did not, recognize any foreign authority.

But not to prolong these remarks, it will be sufficient to say in conclusion, that the language of these documents on the subject of Divine grace and human merit, the distinctness with which they recognise the sole mediation of Christ, and the general tone which pervades them, not only afford convincing evidence of the purity of St. Patrick's faith, but by their harmony with the teaching of the Irish Church of this day vindicate the wisdom of our Reformers.

[7] Mant's History of the Church of Ireland, vol. i. p. 265.

18. The study of these genuine remains of the great missionary, who fourteen centuries ago brought the Gospel here, must convince the members of the Irish Church that their doctrines are not only those of Scripture, but of antiquity; and it cannot but be instructive to those who desire to understand how it is that eminent Divines, bred up in the Church of Rome, nave set on foot the Old Catholic movement,[8] and are gradually working their way back to primitive truth. For they will here find the account of the planting of a Church, such as those distinguished men long for, and which was at the same time Scriptural, National, and Free.

Of the Confessio.

(1.) It was towards the close of his life that he composed the Confessio. His object in writing it was to set before his contemporaries, and to record for the benefit of posterity, the mercies of God to himself, and through him to the Irish nation; to put them in mind of the faith which he had preached, and to impress on their minds that he was influenced only by the Gospel and its promises, to undertake the work of the conversion of the Irish. In doing this, he gives an account of his own conversion; of the obstacles and difficulties which he encountered before and after his entrance on the mission; and answers the charges which had

---

[8] This must be perplexing to those who have always been taught that *Catholic* and *Roman* are identical. But they cannot understand its object, nor appreciate the importance of St. Patrick's writings, until they have learned that the names convey distinct ideas.

been brought against him, one of which was that of
presumption in undertaking such a work, and concludes by reiterating that he had no other motive but
the Gospel and its promises for coming to Ireland.
The importance of this document has been acknowledged
by all who have examined it.   In the words of the
Bishop of Lincoln, " to the Christian generally, especially to the Christian Missionary, and particularly
to those who are engaged in propagating the Gospel in
Ireland, the Confessio of St. Patrick will ever be a work
of deep interest."[9]

The style and manner of this work afford internal
evidence of its genuineness.   "It bears," says Dr.
Neander, " in its simple, rude style, an impress that
corresponds entirely to Patricius' stage of culture.
There are to be found in it none of the traditions which,
perhaps, proceeded only from English monks—nothing
wonderful except what may be very easily explained on
psychological principles.   All this vouches for the
authenticity of the piece."[1]

The absence of miracles is worthy of particular notice.

[9] Ut Supra, sec. iv.

[1] History of the Christian Religion and Church, vol. iii. p. 173, Bohn.
The learned writer appears to mean, not that there is " nothing wonderful" in it, but that it contains no notice of the performance of any
miracles by St. Patrick, and nothing of a miraculous character, (*nichts
wunderbares*,) which does not admit of an explanation.   The allusion
is probably to the dreams mentioned in the Confessio, of which an explanation is now offered on the principles mentioned.   It may be as
well to notice another inaccuracy with respect to St. Patrick in this
translation of Neander, as it seems to contradict the passage above
quoted.   It is said at page 172, "His father gave him a careful
education," which exactly reverses the statement of the original,
" *Keine sorgfältige erziehung.*"

It may possibly be said that St. Patrick refrained from alluding to his gifts from motives of delicacy, yet this would not be according to Apostolic precedent; thus St. Paul did not hesitate to tell the Corinthians, "The signs of an Apostle were wrought among you in all patience, in signs, and wonders, and mighty deeds;"[2] and moreover, this reason will not apply to Secundinus, whose object certainly was to say all that truth permitted in his favour, and who never alludes to miracles.

(2.) A prominent feature in the Confessio is the belief in certain dreams, which he considered of Divine origin. This subject has been already referred to, (p. 16;) and in further explanation it may be observed, that there is nothing to distinguish these from ordinary dreams, which according to the common theory are but our waking thoughts, reproduced in various forms. Thus, what could be more natural than that a captive, languishing for several years in slavery, should have his thoughts occupied about flight, and dream of his escape as he did. (*Confess.* chap. ii. sec. 6.)

" Our dreams (says Professor Stewart) are influenced by the prevailing temper of the mind. . . . Not that this observation holds without exception, but it holds so generally, as must convince us that the state of our spirits has some effect on our dreams, as well as on our waking thoughts. . . . A severe misfortune which has affected the mind deeply, influences our dreams in a similar way, and suggests to us a variety of adventures, analogous in some measure to that event from which

---

[2] 2 Cor. xii. 12.

our distress arises. Such, according to Virgil, were the dreams of the forsaken Dido.[3]

> " Agit ipse furentem
> In somnis Pius Æneas ; semperque relinqui
> Sola sibi—*semper longam incomitata videtur
> Ire viam*, et Tyrios deserta quærere terra."—

(3.) We now come to a passage (chap. ii. sec. 9) which is relied on by some as a proof of his having practised the invocation of saints. If it were not for the exigencies of controversy, and the impossibility of finding any evidence of the practice in his writings, the attempt would probably not have been made, to extract it from this passage, by representing him as praying to an Old Testament Prophet who was never invoked in early times, having been regarded as still alive.[4]

The incident is briefly this : he had a frightful dream, in which Satan seemed to fall on him like a rock, and in his terror he cried out Helias, Helias ; and as he was thus calling out with all his might, the sun rose[5] above the horizon, and he awoke to find it only a dream.

---

[3] Elements of the Philosophy of the Human Mind. D. Stewart, vol. i. p. 335-6.

[4] 2 Kings ii. 11.

[5] The original of the passage is given as follows by Miss Cusack, . 590 :—

Eadem vero (nocte) eram dormiens, et fortiter temptavit me Satanas, quod memor ero quandiu fuero in hoc corpore, et cecidit enim super me veluti saxum ingens, et nihil membrorum prevalens. Sed unde mihi venit in spiritum ut Heliam vocarem, et in hoc vidi in cœlum solem oriri ; et dum clamarem, Heliam, viribus meis, ecce splendor solis illius decidit super me, et statim discussit a me gravitudinem.

Et credo quod a Christo Domino meo [subventus sum et spiritus ejus jam tunc] clamabat pro me.

That one should suffer from nightmare, and call out in his sleep (eram dormiens) is surely not very surprising. If we inquire why he called out Helias, his reply is "he did not know." Obviously, then, this was not the deliberate, conscious act of one uttering a prayer, but an involuntary cry uttered in a dream. But when we turn to the context, it becomes plain that the charge against him is unfounded. "I believe (he says) that I was aided by Christ my Lord, and that His spirit was then crying out on my behalf." Here it is clear that Christ was in his thoughts, and His Spirit, and not one of God's creatures. And it was in this sense the earliest biographers understood him. Thus Probus, "when he had thrice *invoked Christ*, the true Sun, immediately the sun rose upon him, and its light scattered all the mists of darkness, and his strength was restored, and he feared no more the terrors of devils nor their evil designs."[6]

· But what then, it will be asked, is the meaning of the cry Helias, if we abandon, as we must, the far-fetched supposition that he prayed to the Prophet Elias or Elijah? The answer is suggested by two[7] of the lives, which give the word used by him as "Eli," not Elias, from which Dr. Todd infers, with great probability, that the Confessio originally had Eli in the text, which the copyists not understanding, changed to Elias.

[6] The Fifth Life in Colgan, book i. chap. 8. Trias. Th. p. 51, *b*.
[7] In the Second Life, the words are retained in the Irish language, c. 20, ' Ro guidh Eli dia indarput uadh.' "He prayed Eli to expel it (the stone) from him." The Third Life has "Tum Patricius vocavit Eli, in adjutorium suum, trina voce ; venitque Eli et liberavit eum," chap. xvii. As he himself says it was Christ who aided him, it is evident that Eli and Christ must be identical.—Todd, p. 371-3.

. The explanation of the occurrence then appears to be, that in his terror at what he regarded as the presence of Satan in his dream, he called out Eli, *i.e.* My God! more than once, an exclamation not unnatural at such a time.[8]

To use this Hebrew phrase was not habitual with him, and therefore, he says, he did not know why he did it, but it was of course familiar to him as a student of Scripture, who had often meditated on the mysterious cry of his Blessed Master, "Eli, Eli, lama sabachthani."[9]

The coincidence of the rising of the sun with the disappearance of spiritual gloom, has a curious parallel in the following passage of a modern writer. After describing the deep spiritual distress in which he was plunged, from doubts of his acceptance with God, he goes on to say, "About three days after, I was sitting thoughtful in an inner room, and in the multitude of my temptations I imagined that the dull weather might add to my grief; scarce had I thus thought, ere the sun, which had not shone for some time, shined beautifully from the clouds, and the voice of God witnessed at that instant, 'Thus shall the Sun of righteousness arise on thee:' I believed the promise, and found the love of God again shed abroad in my heart."[1]

[8] It will be observed that the words used ("*vocarem*" . . explained further by "*clamarem*") do not really imply an invocation at all ; and this appears to have led Miss Cusack, perhaps unconsciously, to alter the important word when quoting the passage in her Life of St. Patrick. She gives it as follows :—"But how it came into my mind that I should invoke (*Invocarem*) Elias, I know not," p. 143. But when the question is one of doctrine, accuracy is above all things indispensable, though frequently inconvenient.

[9] Matt. xxvii. 46.　　[1] Life of Mr. John Cennick, p. 21, London, 1819.

The Epistle to Coroticus.

(1.) This, though written before the Confessio, is always placed second, perhaps because of its inferior importance. St. Patrick had been a considerable time in Ireland when Coroticus, a Welsh chieftain, and nominally a Christian, landed on the Irish coast at the head of a band of followers, and committed many outrages. Amongst other acts of violence he put to death some converts on the very day of their baptism, others he carried off and sold as slaves ; and when St. Patrick remonstrated by letter, sending also a deputation of the clergy to entreat him to restore some of the plunder and the captives, he dismissed them with ridicule. St. Patrick therefore wrote the Epistle which we now have, " to be given and sent to the soldiers of Coroticus."

(2.) In the two Epistles we find quotations from the Apocrypha, which was read formerly " for example of life and instruction of manners." On the subject of these passages, Archbishop Ussher's observations may be quoted : " Now for those books, true it is that in our Irish and British writers, some of them are alleged as parcels of Scripture, and prophetical writings ; those especially that commonly bear the name of Salomon ; but so also is the fourth book of Esdras, cited by Gildas, in the name of ' blessed Esdras the Prophet ;' which yet our Romanists will not admit to be canonical. Neither do our writers mention any of the rest with more titles of respect than we find given unto them by others of the ancient Fathers, who yet, in express terms, do exclude them out of the number of those books which properly are to be esteemed canonical."[1]

[1] Religion of the Ancient Irish, chap. i.—(Works, vol. iv., p. 249.)

E

The Irish Hymn.

(1.) This remarkable Hymn was first made known to the world by its publication in Dr. Petrie's Essay on Tara Hill. He was led to include it in that valuable work by a mistranslation of the first word—Atomriug—which was supposed to mean "at Tara." This is now known to be an error; but we are indebted to it for a knowledge of the poem, which otherwise would probably for a time longer have slept among the untranslated treasures of ancient Irish literature.

The preface to it in the Book of Hymns states, that it was written "in the time of Loegaire, son of Niall." "Patrick sang it when the ambuscades were set against him by Loegaire, that he might not go to Tara to sow the faith, so that there they seemed before the ambuscaders to be wild deer and a fawn after them, to wit, Benen, and *Faed-fiada* ('guard's cry') is its name."[2] The preaching at Tara was probably the occasion of its composition; but as the preface is of much later date than the poem itself, St. Patrick is not responsible for the legend of the deer, which in all probability arose from the popular mistranslation of Faed-fiada, as "the instruction of the deer."

The prayer in Part II., which seems to aim at enumerating all the possible ways in which the presence of Christ can be sought, has some likeness to a prayer in an Eastern composition known as "The Assemblies of Al Hariri." In the twelfth of these we have the following:—"O God, keep me, in my own land and in my journeying; in my exile and my coming homewards; in my foraging and my return from it; in my trafficking

---

[2] Preface in the Book of Hymns.—Goidelica, p. 151.

and my success from it; in my adventuring and my withdrawing from it;—and guard me in myself and in my property; in my honour and my goods; in my family and my means; in my household and my dwelling; in my strength and my fortune; in my riches and my death," &c. It is in accordance with what has already been said of his training, that his Hymn should thus have a flavour of the East.[3]

(2.) An opinion has been expressed that traces of Pagan error are to be found in this hymn, because it contains a reference to the power of "women, smiths, and Druids," and what seems to be an "invocation of the power of the sky, the sun, fire, lightning, wind, and other created things;"[4] and Dr. Petrie thought that on this account it was formerly regarded as of doubtful orthodoxy, and therefore is not alluded to in the later lives of St. Patrick. But there is no historical evidence for this view; and it seems inconsistent with the fact that, in the seventh century, it was publicly chanted in religious services; and that in the eleventh century the notice prefixed to it in the Book of Hymns was as follows: "Every one who shall sing it every day, with pious meditation on God, demons shall not stay before him; it will be a safeguard to him against every poison and envy," &c; it is further inconsistent with the fact that, in the early part of the present century (according to Dr. Petrie), some portions of it were still remembered by the peasantry and repeated at bed-time as a protection from evil.

[3] "The Assemblies of Al Hariri," (translated by T. Chenery.— Williams and Norgate, 1867,) as referred to by Mr. Stokes, Goidelica, p. 153.
[4] Todd, S. Patrick, p. 430.

Setting aside a fear of the spells of women, (i.e. witches,) &c., a superstition which has only been cast off in modern times by educated people, the question is, whether the writer addressed prayer to any but Father, Son, and Spirit.   Now, in the first place, it is certain that he preached against sun-worship,[5] and that he was careful to give no sanction to idolatrous practices ;[6] and even this hymn presents Christian truth in strong contrast with pagan error, his antagonism to which is evident in the very stanza (vi.) which contains the words, " so have I invoked all these virtues between me and these." It is, therefore, very improbable that his views were tinged with that class of superstition : but if not, how is this language to be understood ?   What meaning must be attached to the word "invoke," which will harmonize with St. Patrick's known opinions and with the hymn as a whole ?   On looking at the structure of the poem we find it consists of two parts ; the first has five verses, in which he " binds himself to" certain virtues :—

1. To the virtue of an Invocation of the Trinity.
2. To the virtue of certain events in the life of Christ.
3. To the virtue of the obedience of God's servants.
4. To the virtue of certain qualities of matter.
5. To the virtue of certain attributes of God.

There is here, properly speaking, no prayer.   The formula, "I bind myself to," is not a prayer.   This will appear more clearly by comparing the expressions in stanza ii. with the prayer to Christ in the Second Part.   Thus, in the former we read, "I bind myself to the virtue of Christ's birth ;" in the latter, " Christ protect me to-day."   The former is concerned with

---

[5] Confess., chap. v. sec. 24.   [6] Ibid., chap. ii. sec. 9.

things; the latter is a direct prayer to a personal Christ.

The meaning of the expression, " I bind myself to," appears to be, " I connect myself with, or claim to have on my side," these virtues or powers.

The conclusion then appears to be, that, regarding all evil—moral, intellectual, and physical—as springing from the agency of demoniac powers, which were obedient to spells and incantations, he felt himself, on the other hand, in intimate union with One who was not only the Creator, but the Ruler of all things, and the immediate source of all the operations of nature.

Thus the key to the understanding of the hymn is, probably, Heb. xii. 22-24, with 1 Cor. iii. 21-23. As a Christian, with a vivid sense of the reality of his privileges, he felt that he was brought into union with an innumerable company of angels, with the general assembly and church of the first-born, with God, the judge of all, with the spirits of just men made perfect, and with Jesus, the mediator of the new covenant. " All things worked together for good to him ;" all things, in fact, were " his." Though Druids muttered their incantations, and witches wove their spells, they could not touch him, for the powers of nature were on his side, not on their's; and now he claims his privileges, and " binds himself" to them all.

It is the " Guard's Cry," as, in the presence of danger he falls back on his supports, and unites himself to them.

In connection with this subject, it may be mentioned that in the attempt to represent St. Patrick as practising the invocation of saints, this hymn has been pressed

into the service. " The saint (it is said) invokes or
prays for the help, (*virtute*,) virtue, of the blessed
Trinity, the angels, and the saints, in his great undertaking ;"[7] but the answer is supplied by another note
in the next page, which runs thus : " It has been
thought that the saint invoked the power of the sun, as
he had invoked the power or virtue of the angels, apostles, and virgins."[8]   To this there is no reply, but that
he, as " a Catholic missionary, who had come to convert a nation from idolatry," *could not* have done so.
Nevertheless, it is quite clear that if he prayed to the
saints he must also have prayed to the sun, for his
language is the same with respect to both.

Secundinus's Hymn.

The author of this poem, who was otherwise known
by his Irish name of Sechnall, is thus noticed in an
ancient Irish manuscript,[9] belonging probably to the
ninth or tenth century :—

" Sechnall, viz., the son of Restitutus, was he who made this Hymn
in honour of Patrick, for he was a disciple of Patrick, and he was also
the son of Patrick's sister, (*i.e.*, Liamania,) and he was of the Longo-
bards, (Lombards,) of Letha, as Eochaidh O'Flannagan has said—

> Sechnall, son of Ua Baird, the gifted,
> The most gifted of living men ;
> Of the race of the pure, fierce, white-coloured
> Longobards of Leatha. "

[7] Miss Cusack's Life of St. Patrick, p. 264, note.   The insertion of
the Latin word *virtute* here is superfluous, as the original is Irish.
[8] Ibid, p. 265, note.
[9] The Leabhar Breac, now in the library of the Royal Irish Academy.

He came to Ireland, A.D. 439, to assist St. Patrick in his missionary labours, and appears to have been entrusted by him with the charge of his duties at Armagh, during his absence in other parts of Ireland. He resided chiefly at Dunshaughlin,[1] which derives its name from him, and, according to the Annals of the Four Masters, his death took place A.D. 467, many years before that of St. Patrick.

He composed this hymn in praise of St. Patrick,[2] whose success in organizing the Irish Church was then apparent ; and its peculiar interest lies in its being a description of him by an eyewitness, who had the best possible means of knowing the truth, and committed his impressions to writing, at the time when the subject of his praise was still actively engaged in his missionary work. It will be observed that he speaks throughout in the present tense.

The story of the origin of the poem is given as follows by the author of the Preface to the Hymn, whose name and date are unknown :—

Secundinus was one day engaged in conversation

---

[1] Domhnach-Sechnaill, the Dominica or Church of Sechnall, corrupted to Dunshaughlin.

[2] *Hymni Sti. Patritii Magistri Scotorum.* This is the title in the Antiphonary of Bangor. In the Book of Hymns it is *Episcopi Scotorum.* Perhaps different aspects of his work are intended by the titles, for, in executing his office as a Bishop in the evangelizing of the Irish people, it was necessary for him to be also a Teacher, and to impart to them the rudiments of secular learning. This seems to be the inference from the statement in the Book of Armagh, " He used to baptize men daily, and read letters and abgatoriæ (alphabets) with them." This was the alphabet then in use on the continent of Europe, which became in their hands the key to unlock the treasures of foreign learning.

with some holy men on the subject of St. Patrick's character and labours. They praised him highly; but Secundinus said, "He would be the best of men if he had not too little preached charity," meaning that if he had preached a pious liberality, more lands and posses- sions would have been contributed by the ready devo- tion of the people for the maintenance and endowment of churches. The conversation having come to the ears of St. Patrick, "who was eminent for true charity," he replied, "It is for the sake of charity that I preach charity so sparingly," explaining that he feared to pre- judice the future Church by being too exacting in his demands. Secundinus acknowledged his error, and having asked forgiveness, a reconciliation ensued, and he then composed this hymn.

This story is by no means improbable, as St. Patrick's disinterestedness was one of those features of his character which would attract attention, and seem to be open to the charge of imprudence.[3] But whether this is so or not, the interest of the hymn is very great. The references given by the editor at each verse will show that the mind of the writer was completely imbued with a knowledge of Holy Scripture, from which most of the thoughts and expressions in the hymn are drawn.

[3] Confess., ch. v. 21, 22.

THE EPISTLES OF ST. PATRICK.

BOOK I.

THE CONFESSIO.[1]

CHAPTER I.

OF ST. PATRICK'S BIRTH AND CAPTIVITY, AND OF THIS CONFESSIO.

I, PATRICK,[2] a sinner, the rudest and the least of all the faithful, and an object of the greatest contempt to many, am the son of Calpornius, a deacon, the son of the late Potitus, a presbyter,[3]

---

[1] *Confessio.* The word, Confession, does not adequately express the meaning of the Latin here. The words *Fateor, Confiteor, Confessio,* appear to be used in these Epistles in the sense of "Declaration." Thus, Confess. sec. 2, "We should exalt and confess (*confiteremur*) his wonders;" and perhaps this is derived from the passage quoted from Tobit, "It is honourable to reveal and confess (*confiteri*) the works of God." See also Epistle to Coroticus, sec. 1, note 1. It seems better, to avoid ambiguity, to leave the word untranslated.

[2] *Patricius.* It is not necessary to suppose that this title was given to him by any one, for at this time, according to Gibbon, "The meanest subjects of the Roman Empire assumed the *illustrious* name of *Patricius,* which, by the conversion of Ireland, has been communicated to a whole nation."—*Decline and Fall,* vol. vi. p. 229, note, ed. London, 1806.

[3] *A presbyter.* See Introduction, p. 13.

Patrick, a
Briton,

who lived in Bannaven, a village of Tabernia,[4] in
the neighbourhood of which he had a small farm ;
and here I was taken captive.[5] I was then nearly
sixteen years old; I was ignorant of the true

carried away
into Ireland
at sixteen
years of age,

God, and was brought to Ireland in captivity,
with so many thousand persons, as we deserved,
because we had turned away from God,[6] and had
not kept His commandments, and were disobe-
dient to our priests, who admonished us of our

(2 Chron.
xxix. 10.)

salvation ; and the Lord brought on us "the
anger of His fury," and scattered us among many

---

[4] *Bannaven Tabernia.*   Dr. Lanigan (Ecc. Hist.) thinks
this was Bononia, now Boulogne, in France, and supports his
opinion with much learning and ingenuity ; but his arguments
are not satisfactory ; and a passage occurs in the Confession,
(ch. iv. sec. 19,) where Britain, his native land, is distinguished
from Gaul, and the two countries spoken of in their relative
positions to Ireland, in such a way as to indicate that Great
Britain is intended.   See also ch. ii. sec. 8, note, and Introduction, p. 12.

[5] These expeditions from Ireland, in one of which he was
taken captive, appear to have been annual.   "Anniversarias
prædas trans maria exaggerabant."— *Gildas,* chap. xiv.   Gibbon, generally slow to believe where Irish matters are concerned, assents to this—" We may believe that, in one of these
Irish inroads, the future apostle was led away captive."—*Decline and Fall,* v. 228, ed. London, 1808.

[6] As a specimen of the way in which the popular lives are
written, the following may be quoted :—"And the boy Patrick
grew up precious in the sight of the Lord, in the old age of
wisdom, and in the ripeness of virtue.   And the number of his
merits multiplied beyond the number of his years : the afflu-
ence of all holy charities overflowed in the breast of the boy,
and all the virtues, met together, made their dwelling in his
youthful body."—*Life of St. Patrick, Patron, Primate, and
Apostle of Ireland.*   Dublin : J. Duffy, 1838, p. 43.   This account is the very contrary of what he gives of himself.

nations, even to the uttermost parts of the earth, where now my littleness is seen, amongst a foreign people. And there the Lord brought me to a *and there enlightened by God,* sense of my unbelief, that I might, even at a late season, call my sins to remembrance, and turn with all my heart to the Lord my God, who regarded my low estate, and, taking pity on my youth and ignorance, guarded me, before I understood anything, or had learned to distinguish between good and evil, and strengthened and comforted me as a father does his son.

Sec. 2. Wherefore I am unable, and indeed I *confesses the goodness of God* ought not, to be silent respecting the many blessings, and the large measure of grace which the Lord vouchsafed to bestow on me in the land of my captivity; for this is the only recompense which is in our power, that after being chastened and brought to know God, we should exalt and confess his wonders before every nation under heaven; that—

There[7] is no other God, nor ever was, nor will *and his own faith.* be hereafter, except God the Father, unbegotten,

---

[7] It has been objected to this Creed that it attributes the creation of all things to the Son; (Richey, Lectures on History of Ireland, p. 37;) but the objector must surely have forgotten that the Nicene Creed does the same, and in this both follow Holy Scripture—see Heb. i.; John i. The office of Christ, the Word of God, in the creation and government of the world, is an undoubted truth of Revelation. "His mediatorial function in the Church is represented as flowing from his mediatorial function in the world." This truth, so often forgotten, and here brought prominently forward, throws light on the so-called invocation of the powers of nature in the Irish Hymn. This confession of faith resembles the Nicene Creed,

without beginning; From whom is all beginning; Who upholds all things as we have said : And his Son Jesus Christ, whom we acknowledge to have been always with the Father; Who before the beginning of the world was spiritually present with the Father; Begotten in an unspeakable manner before all beginning; By whom were made all .things visible and invisible; Who was (Rev. lii. 21.) made man, and having overcome death was received into heaven to the Father: And he hath given him a name which is above every name: that at the name of Jesus every knee should bow of things in heaven and things in earth and things under the earth, and that every tongue should (Philip. ii. 9-11.) confess that Jesus Christ is Lord and God :[8] In whom we believe, and we await his coming, who ere long shall judge the quick and dead : Who will render to every one according to his deeds, and has poured out abundantly on us the gift of the Holy Spirit, even the earnest of immortality, who makes those that believe and obey, to be the sons of God the Father, and joint-heirs with

but has fewer articles, and is more copious on the Divinity of our Lord. Its close adherence to Holy Scripture, and the entire absence of those errors which are embodied in the present Creed of the Roman Catholic Church, have been pointed out in the Introduction, pp. 36-40.

It follows plainly, from the comparison there instituted, that any Roman Catholic who believes his to be the ancient faith, out of which no one can be saved, must hold that St. Patrick was excluded from salvation. The omission of the Virgin Mary's name is remarkable.

[8] *Lord and God.* The reading differs somewhat from the Authorised Version and the Vulgate.

Christ; Whom we confess and adore—one God in the Trinity of the sacred name.

For he himself has said by the Prophet, "Call upon me in the day of trouble and I will deliver thee, and thou shalt glorify me;" and again he (Psalm l. 15.) says, "It is honourable to reveal and confess the works of God."[9] (Tob. xii. 7.)

Sec. 3. Although I am imperfect in many things, I wish my brethren and relatives[1] to know And meditates a true my disposition, that they may be able to perceive confession the desire of my soul. I am not ignorant of the testimony of my Lord, who declares in the Psalm, "Thou shalt destroy them that speak leasing" (Psalm v. 6.) [falsehood]; and again, "The mouth that belieth slayeth the soul;" and the same Lord says (Wis. i. 11.) in the Gospel, "Every idle word that men shall speak, they shall give account thereof in the day of judgment." Therefore, I ought in great fear (Matt. xii. 36.) and trembling, to dread this sentence on that day when no one shall be able to withdraw or hide himself, but all must give an account even of the least sins before the judgment-seat of Christ the Lord. And for this reason, although I have for some time meditated writing, I have hesitated about himself to write, until now; for I feared falling upon the language of men, because I have not studied like others who have enjoyed the great advantages of becom-

---

[9] *It is honourable.* On this and other quotations from the Apocrypha, see Archbishop Ussher's Observations. Introduction, p. 49.

[1] *Brethren and relatives.* Who had opposed his coming to Ireland.

ing acquainted with the Holy Scriptures in both ways equally,[2] and have never changed their language from infancy, but have rather always approached to perfection ; for I have to translate my thoughts and speech into a foreign language.[3]

Sec. 4. And it can be easily proved from the style of my writing, how I am instructed and learned in discourses, "for (says the Wise Man) by speech understanding is known, and learning, and the doctrine of truth." But what does it avail to offer an excuse, however true, especially when accompanied with presumption ? Since I now in my old age attempt what I did not attain in my youth, for my sins[4] prevented me from confirming what I had not before [my conversion] thoroughly examined. But, who believes me ? and yet to repeat what I stated before, I was taken captive when a youth, nay, rather, when almost a beardless boy, before I knew what I ought to seek or to avoid. Wherefore, at this day I am greatly ashamed and afraid to expose my unskilfulness, because I am unable to explain

margin note: although with some hesitation

margin note: (Ecclus. iv. 24.)

margin note: on account of his uncultivated style.

---

[2] *Both ways equally.* " In the Greek as well as in the Latin version, or in the version of Jerome as well as in the old Italic."—*O'Conor.*

[3] *Foreign language.* The consciousness of his inability to write with purity and correctness had hitherto deterred him, for " whatever knowledge of Latin he possessed was very much impaired by the admixture of the Irish language."—*Tillemont.*

[4] *Sins.* He appears to mean that his sinful neglect of divine things in early youth, had unfitted him then and long afterwards for bearing witness to the truth, that "the Gospel is the power of God unto salvation."

myself with clearness and brevity of speech, as
the Spirit greatly desires, and all the feelings of
my mind suggest. But if I had been gifted like
others, I would not have been silent, inasmuch
as a recompense was due from me. Perhaps,
there are some who think that in this I put myself forward, although I am ignorant and slow
of speech, but [they should remember that] it is
written, " The tongue of the stammerers shall
quickly learn to speak peace,"[5] and how much (Isai. xxxii.
4.)
more ought we to attempt [this work] " who
(says he) are the epistle of Christ (who was set (Acts xiii.
47.)
for salvation unto the ends of the earth) written
in your hearts, if not eloquently, yet powerfully
and enduringly, not with ink, but with the Spirit (2 Cor. iii. 2,
3.)
of the living God."

Sec. 5. And, again, the Spirit testifies, "Hus-
bandry was ordained by the Most High." Where- (Ecclus. vii.
15.)
fore,[6] at the first, I [undertook this work] though
a rustic, a fugitive, and moreover, unlearned and
incapable of providing against the future, but
this I know most certainly, that—especially before I was humbled—I was like a stone that lay
in the deep mire, and He, who alone is powerful,

[5] *Peace.* The Authorised Version and the Vulgate have
"plainly."

[6] *Wherefore.* The connexion seems to be : "supported by
passages of Scripture, and the reasons mentioned, I over-
came the feeling of unfitness for preaching the Gospel, which
my imperfect education and unpolished manners gave rise to
in my mind at the outset, and I now feel justified in repressing
similar feelings respecting the Confessio, by similar arguments."

That he
might not be
ungrateful to
God,
came, and in his own mercy, raised me, and
lifted me up, and placed me on the top of the
wall,[7] from which it is my duty to cry aloud, in
order to make some recompense to the Lord for
all the benefits temporal and eternal, beyond
man's conception, which he has bestowed upon
me. But, wherefore, do you wonder, O great
and small, who fear God ? and you, rhetoricians[8] of the Gauls, who know not the Lord ?
Hear, then, and inquire who has stirred me up,
who am a fool, out of the midst of those who are
esteemed wise and skilled in law, and powerful
in eloquence, and in everything, and inspired
beyond others (if haply it be so) me, the object
by Whom he
was so
greatly
exalted.
of this world's hatred ?   [It was God] provided
that if I were worthy, I should, during my life,
faithfully labour with fear and reverence and

---

[7] *Top of the wall.* Granted to him the high privilege of
proclaiming the Gospel to the Irish people. The reader will
notice the allusion to the description of Christians as " lively
stones" forming the spiritual house of God.—1 Peter, ii. 5 ;
Ephesians, ii. 21, 22. Nothing can be more opposed to the
Roman Catholic doctrine of merit than this passage.

[8] *Rhetoricians.* We may gather from the context that some
of these men, who, as he tells us, were esteemed wise, and
learned, and eloquent, had expressed astonishment that Patrick
should undertake an office for which, in their eyes, he was so
ill-fitted ; to this, he replies with St. Paul, 1 Corinthians, i.
26-29. Gaul was famous in early times for its rhetoricians
and pleaders ; Juvenal, who wrote in the first century, alludes
to it, as—

" Gallia, vel potius nutricula causidicorum,
        Africa "—*Satire*, vii. 148,

And again,

" Gallia causidicos docuit facunda Britannos."—*Satire*, xv. 11.

without murmuring, for the good of the nation
to which the love of Christ transferred and gave
me, in fine, that I should serve them with
humility and truth.

CHAPTER II.

HAVING ESCAPED FROM SLAVERY BY FLIGHT,
HE RETURNS TO HIS COUNTRY.

(Rom. xii. 3.) SEC. 6. In "the measure, therefore, of the faith" of the Trinity,[1] it is my duty to make a distinction [of persons] without regarding any censure (2 Thess. ii 16.) of danger; to make known "the gift of God," and "everlasting consolation," and to proclaim the name of God everywhere, faithfully and fearlessly, that after my death I may leave [the For whom he writes this. knowledge of it] to my Gallican brethren,[2] and my sons whom I have baptized in the Lord, many thousands in number. And I was neither worthy nor deserving that the Lord should so favour me, the least of his servants, as after such great afflictions and difficulties, after captivity, after many years, to grant me so large a measure of his grace for the conversion of this nation, [a blessing] which, in my youth, I never either hoped or thought of.

But after I had come to Ireland,[3] I was em-

---

[1] I believe in a Threeness, with confession of an Oneness, in the Creator of the Universe.—*St. Patrick's Hymn.*

[2] *Gallican brethren.* The persons whom he brought with him from Gaul, to assist in preaching the Gospel to the Irish.

[3] *Hiberionem.* Ireland is called by this name in the Itinerary of Antoninus also.

ployed every day in tending sheep, and I used often in the day to have recourse to prayer, and *While in slavery he is greatly devoted to prayer,* the love of God was thus growing stronger and stronger, and the fear of Him and faith were increasing, and the Spirit, so that in a single day I have said as many as a hundred prayers, and in the night almost as many; and I used to remain even in the woods and on the mountain,[4] and used to rise to prayer before daylight, in the midst of snow, and ice, and rain, and I felt no injury from it, nor was there any sloth in me; because, as I now see, the spirit was then fervent within me. And there one night, in a dream, I *and is admonished of his deliverance.* heard a voice saying to me, " Thou dost well to fast, and shalt soon return to thy country;" and again, after a little time, I heard a response saying to me, " Behold, thy ship is ready;" and the place[5] was not near, but perhaps two hundred miles off, and I had never been there, nor was I acquainted with any one there.

Sec. 7. And after this I took flight; and having left the man with whom I had been six years, *He flees, trusting in God.* I came in the strength of the Lord, who directed my way to good; and I feared nothing until I arrived at the ship; and, on the day of my arrival, the ship had moved out from her berth, and I spoke to them, saying I had money to pay for

---

[4] *Mountain.* Slemish, (Sliabh Mis,) in the county of Antrim, near which his master lived.

[5] *The place.* It is useless to attempt to decide what port this was.

my passage with them ;[6] and the master[7] was
displeased, and replied angrily, "Don't at all
think to go with us;" and when I heard this, I
withdrew from them, to go to the cottage where I
was lodging; and on my way I began to pray,
and before I finished my prayer I heard one of
them crying out loudly after me, "Come back at
once, for those men are calling you ;" and I returned immediately to them, and they began to
say to me, "Come, for we receive you in good
faith ; make friends with us in what manner you
please." And then I gave up the thought of fleeing, on account of the fear of God, yet I hoped
they would [before long] say to me, "Come in
the faith of Jesus Christ," because they were
Gentiles. And when I had thus obtained my
desire, we immediately set sail.

    Sec. 8. After three days we arrived at land,

and is ad-mitted into a ship by the sailors.

---

    [6] *Ut haberem unde navigarem cum illis.* This is contrary,
however, to the statement of Probus, who says (lib. i. ch. iv.)
they would not admit him because he could not pay for his
passage. The Book of Armagh gives *abirem* for *haberem*, the
meaning of which might be that he would go to some point
from which he could embark, as the ship was already under
sail. Allowing the former, however, to be the correct reading,
the master may have refused to receive him, knowing him to
be a fugitive slave ; for, according to the Irish bards, the
distinction of ranks in Ireland was indicated by the colours
of the dress long before the Christian era. Keating says,
"Tighernmhas established it as a custom in Ireland, that there
should be *only one colour in the clothing of a bondman*, two in
that of a plebeian, three in that of a soldier," &c. —*Forus Feasa
air Eirin*, at the year A.M. 2811.
    [7] *Master.* He seems to have been a kind of supercargo, and
to have had but a temporary connexion with the ship.

and for twenty-eight days[8] we journeyed through a desert; when, their provisions becoming exhausted, they suffered severely from hunger; and one day the master said to me: "What do you say, Christian? your God is great and all-powerful; can you not then pray for us, since we are in danger of perishing by famine, for it is very improbable that we shall ever see the face of man again." And I plainly said to them: "Turn faithfully and with your whole heart to the Lord our God—for to him nothing is impossible—that he may send food into your path to-day, even until you are satisfied, for it abounds everywhere to him." And, with God's help, it happened so; for lo, a herd of swine appeared in the way before our eyes, and they killed many of them, and remained there two nights, much refreshed; and they were relieved [from hunger] by their flesh, for many of the party had sunk from exhaustion, and were left scarcely alive by the way-side. After this they gave the greatest thanks to God, and I was honoured in their eyes.

When they afterwards suffer from hunger in the desert,

he obtains food for them by his prayers,

. Sec. 9. And from that day forth they had food in abundance. They also found wild honey, and

---

[8] *Twenty-eight days.* This fact is fatal to Dr. Lanigan's supposition that Boulogne was the native city of St. Patrick. If it were so, and if the party were going there, the easiest course would have been to sail directly to Boulogne; yet, according to him, they sailed to Treguier, in Normandy, and then, at the risk of their lives, travelled for twenty-eight days through a wilderness, where there were no provisions obtainable, to reach a port which was little farther from them, in the first instance, than that to which they sailed.

offered part of it to me; and one of them said,

and is delivered from the assault of Satan, "This is offered in sacrifice[9] thanks to God;" after that I tasted no more. But the same night, while I was asleep, Satan, of whom[1] I will be mindful as long as I shall be in this body, tempted me strongly, and fell on me like a great rock, so that I was unable to move my limbs; but I know not how it came into my mind to call Helias,[2] and at this moment I saw the sun rise in the heavens, and while I was crying out, Helias, Helias, with all my might, behold, the splendour of the sun fell upon me, and immediately removed all the weight; and I believe by the power of Christ. that I was aided by Christ my Lord, and that his Spirit was then crying out in my behalf; and I hope it will be so in the day of my adversity, even as the Lord says in the Gospel, "It is not ye that speak, but the Spirit of your Father which (Matt. x. 20.) speaketh in you." Not many years after I was again[8] taken captive; and, on the first night that

---

[9] *Offered in sacrifice.* This referred to the honey which the heathen offered in sacrifice to his God. The conduct of St. Patrick here proves that the Scriptures were "a lamp unto his feet, and a light unto his path;" for, in refusing to taste any more food on this occasion, he evidently had in mind the injunction of St. Paul—1 Corinthians x. 28, 29.

[1] *Of whom,* '*cujus.*'—See 1 Pet. v. 8; Another reading is, *quod,* 'which,' referring to the temptation.

[2] *Helias.* See Introduction, pp. 46-48. It has been well remarked by Dr. Mason, that they who suppose St. Patrick here to have invoked Elias, make the same mistake as the Jews when they said of our Lord, "Behold, he calleth Elias."

[8] The reading of the original is here uncertain; and it was probably his enforced stay with the sailors which he regarded as a captivity.

I remained with them,[4] I heard a divine response saying to me, " You shall be two months with them ;" and it happened so, for on the sixtieth night the Lord delivered me out of their hands. Behold, in the journey he provided for us food, and fire, and dry weather, daily, until on the fourteenth day we came to men. As I have above mentioned, we journeyed for twenty-eight days through a desert ; and, on the night when we arrived at the abodes of men, we had no provisions remaining.

[4] *i.e.*, the captors.

· CHAPTER III.

OF HIS CALLING INTO IRELAND, AND OF MANY IMPEDIMENTS.

SEC. 10. And again, after a few years, I was in Britain[1] with my parents, who received me as a son, and besought me earnestly that then at least, after so great tribulations as I had endured, I should not go away from them any more. And there I saw in a vision of the night, a man whose name was Victoricus,[2] coming as if from Ireland with innumerable letters, one of which he handed to me, and I read the beginning of the letter, which ran thus, "The voice of the people of Ireland ;" and while I was reading aloud the beginning of the letter, I thought at that very moment I heard the voice of those who were near the Wood of Foclud,[3] which is by the Western Sea,[4] and they cried out thus as if with one voice, "We entreat thee, holy youth, to come and henceforth walk among us." And I was very

After another captivity,

being invited to Ireland by a dream,

[1] *Britanniis.* The word is in the plural, as including all the islands near Britain.

[2] *Victoricus.* From this simple incident has originated the fable of an angel called Victor, who held frequent conversations with him, and directed him as to his proceedings.— *Lanigan,* i. 144.

This name, the "Conquering One," was an omen of success in his missionary labours.—See Rev. vi. 2.

[3] *Foclud.* This wood was situated in and near the parish of Killala, barony of Tirawley, and county of Mayo.

[4] *Western Sea.* The Atlantic Ocean.

much pricked to the heart, and could read no more, and so I awoke. Thanks be to God, that after very many years the Lord has granted to them according to their cry.

Sec. 11. And on another night [some one,] I know not, God knows, whether in me or near me, spoke in most eloquent language, which I heard and could not understand, except that at *and by an inward voice,* the end of the speech he addressed me thus, "Who for thee laid down his life?" and so I *(1 John iii. 16.)* awoke full of joy, and again I saw one praying in me, and I was as it were within my body, and I heard him over me, that is, over the inner man, and there he prayed fervently with groanings, and during this time I was full of astonishment, and was wondering and considering who it could be that was praying in me; but at the end of the prayer he declared that it was The Spirit; and so I awoke, and remembered that the Apostle says, "The Spirit also helpeth the infirmity of our prayer, for we know not what we should pray for as we ought, but the Spirit itself maketh intercession for us with groanings which cannot be uttered," that is, expressed in words : *(Rom. viii. 26.)* and again, "The Lord our Advocate makes intercession for us." And when I was sorely tried *(1 John ii. 1.)* by some of my elders,[5] who came and [spoke of] my sins as an objection to my laborious episcopate; on that day in particular I was almost driven to fall away, not only for a time, but for

---

[5] *Elders.* His elder relatives and friends.—*Lanigan.*

eternity; but the Lord spared a pilgrim and a stranger; and for the honour of his name he in his mercy powerfully succoured me in this severe *he over-comes trials* affliction, because I was not entirely deserving of censure as regards the blame and disgrace now brought on me. I pray God they may not be accounted guilty of the sin of laying stumbling-*(Rev. ii. 14.)* blocks [in a brother's way.] After thirty years they found me, and charged against me the word which I confessed before I was deacon.

Sec. 12. From anxiety of mind, I told my dearest friend in sorrow what I had done in my boyhood one day, nay, rather one hour, because *anxieties,* I was not yet used to overcome [temptation.] I know not, God knows, if I was then fifteen years of age, and from my childhood I was not a believer in the true God, but continued in death and unbelief until I was severely chastened; and in truth I have been humbled by hunger and nakedness, and on the other hand, I did not come to Ireland of my own desire,[6] nor until I was almost worn out; but this proved rather a benefit to me, for thus I was corrected by the Lord, and he rendered me fit to be at this day what was once far from my thoughts, so that I should interest or concern myself for the salvation of others, for at that time I had no thoughts even about myself. And in the night succeeding the day when I was reproved by being reminded of the things above mentioned, I saw in a vision

---

[6] *Non sponte pergebam.* He always attributes his mission to a Divine call. See ch. v. sec. 20.

of the night my name written against me[7] without a title of honour, and meanwhile I heard a Divine response, saying to me, "We have seen with displeasure the face of the [Bishop] elect, and his name stripped of its honours." He did not say thus, "Thou hast seen," but, "We have seen with displeasure," as if he there joined himself with me ; even as he has said, "He that toucheth you toucheth the apple of my eye." (Zech ii. 8.) Therefore I give thanks to him who has comforted me in all things, that he did not hinder me from *obstructions,* the journey which I had proposed, and also as regards my work which I had learned of Christ. But on the contrary, I felt no small power from him, and my faith was approved before God and men.

Sec. 13. Wherefore I say boldly, I fear no reproaches of conscience now or hereafter. God is my witness, that I have not lied in what I have stated to you, but I feel the more grieved that my dearest friend,[8] whom I trusted even with my *and wrongs.*

[7] *Scriptum erat contra faciem meam.* On this obscure passage the Bollandists say, "There seems to be an allusion here to some book against the mission of St. Patrick, in which 'his name being stripped of its honours,' he was simply designated Patrick, without any title of honour or mark of episcopal dignity."—*Acta Sanctorum,* March 17. But perhaps a more probable conjecture would be that he saw in his dream a picture of his own face, with the name Patrick written opposite. It is said that pictures with the names of all the objects written opposite, still exist in the Greek monasteries, and that many of them are as old as the fifth century. See Preface to Curzon's Monasteries of the Levant. It is also usual on ancient coins.

[8] *Dearest friend.* The Bollandists suppose this to mean Germanus, Bishop of Auxerre.

life [should have been the cause] of my being
rewarded with such a response; and I learned
from some brethren, that before that defence,[9] on
an occasion when I was not present, and when I
was not in Britain, and with which I had nothing
to do, he defended me in my absence. He had
also said to me with his own mouth, "You are
to be raised to the rank of Bishop." What
could have influenced him that he should afterwards, before all, good and bad, publicly throw
discredit on me with respect to an office which
he had before spontaneously and gladly offered?
There is a Lord who is greater than all—I have
said enough. But yet I ought not to hide the
gift of God, which was given me in the land of
my captivity: because I sought him earnestly
then, and I found him there, and he preserved
me from all iniquities; so I believe, "because of
his Spirit that dwelleth in me," and has worked
in me even to this day; God knows if it were
man who had spoken to me,[1] I would perhaps
have been silent for the love of Christ.

Sec. 14. Wherefore I give unceasing thanks

the authors of which he pardons,

(Rom. viii. 11 —margin.)

---

[9] *Defensionem illam.* Perhaps he means that some prohibi-
tion was laid on him, for the Gauls used the word "'defendo'
and its derivatives in that sense."—*Bollandists.*

[1] *Spoken to me.* i.e., in the vision before mentioned. His
meaning seems to be, that if one of his brethren had called
his attention to the indignity offered to him in depriving his
name of its honour, he would not have noticed it, remember-
ing the example of his Master, Christ, but in consequence of
his dream, he now looked on it as an indignity offered to
Christ in the person of one of his servants.

to God, who preserved me faithful in the day of my temptation, so that I can this day confidently offer up my soul as " a living sacrifice" to Christ *in all things giving* my Lord, who preserved me from all my trou- *thanks to God,* bles ;[2] so that I may say, " Who am I, O Lord, or what is my calling, that thou hast laboured together with me with such Divine power ?" So *(1 Cor. iii. 9.)* that at this day I can constantly rejoice among the nations, and magnify thy name wherever I may be, not only in prosperity, but in adversity, [teaching me] that I ought to accept with a con- *(Phil. iv. 11, 12)* tented mind whatever may befall me, whether good or evil, and always give thanks to God, who *who manifested himself to him.* showed me that I should believe in him for ever without doubting, and who heard me that al- *(Eph. v. 20.)* though I am ignorant, I should in these last days attempt to undertake so holy and wonderful a work, so that I should imitate those who the Lord long since foretold should preach his Gospel "for a witness to all nations" before the *(Matt. xxiv. 14.)* end of the world ; which has been so accomplished as we have seen. Behold we are witnesses, because the Gospel has been preached to the limits of human habitation.

---

[2] *Troubles.* St. Patrick is reckoned among the martyrs in the Book of Obits of Christ Church, Dublin, and his claim to the title is thus explained in Colgan : " Nor is he unfitly called a martyr who evermore bore the cross of Christ in his soul and body ; who, continually warring with Druids, with idolatrous kings and chieftains, and with demons, exposed his body to a thousand kinds of death, and had a heart always ready to endure them, thus presenting himself a living sacrifice to the Lord."—*Trias. Thaum.* p. 168.

See History of Dairi and his gift, Introduction, pp. 25, 26.

CHAPTER IV.

THE FRUITS OF HIS MISSION.

SEC. 15. But it is long to detail the particulars
of my labours even partially. I will briefly say
how the God of piety often liberated me from
slavery; how he delivered me from twelve dangers by which my soul was perilled, besides many
snares and troubles which I cannot enumerate,
nor will I do injustice to my readers; [yet I cannot altogether be silent], while I have a Master
who knows all things even before they come to
pass, as he does me a poor helpless creature.
Therefore, the Divine response frequently admonished me [to consider] whence I derived this
wisdom, which was not in me, who neither knew
the number of my days nor was acquainted with
God; whence I obtained afterwards so great and
salutary a gift as to know or to love God, and
also that I should give up my home and parents.
And many offers were made to me with weeping
and tears, and I incurred displeasure there from
some of my elders, contrary to my wish; but
under the guidance of God I in no way consented,
nor gave way to them; yet not I, but the grace of
God which prevailed in me, and resisted them all,
in order that I might come to preach the Gospel

He praises God, who preserved him from sins,

and be-stowed on him the grace of preaching.

to the people of Ireland,[1] and bear with the ill-treatment of the unbelieving, and that I should be reproached as a foreigner, and have to endure many persecutions, even to bonds, and that I should give up my free birth for the good of others.

Sec. 16. And I am ready at this moment to lay down even my life with joy for his name's sake, if I shall be worthy, and thus I wish to bestow it even unto death, if the Lord should so favour me. Because I am greatly a debtor to God, who has bestowed his grace so largely upon me that multitudes should be born again to God through me, and afterwards confirmed,[2] and that of these, clergy should be everywhere ordained for a people lately coming to the faith, whom the Lord took from the extremities of the earth, as he promised long before by his Prophets—" The Gentiles shall come unto thee from the ends of the earth, and shall say, Surely our fathers have inherited lies, vanity, and things wherein there is no profit;" and again, " I have set thee to be a light of the Gentiles, that thou shouldst be for salvation unto the ends of the earth;", and thus I wish to await the promise of him who in truth never deceives, which is thus given in the Gospel—" They shall come from the east and west,

and zeal to propagate the Gospel,

and to bring the Gentiles to Christ,

(Jer. xvi. 19.)

(Acts xiii. 47.)

---

[1] *Hibernas gentes.* The Irish nations, or tribes.

[2] *Postmodum consummarentur.* These words are not in the copy of the Confessio in the Book of Armagh. The word *consummare* was used in the sense of confirmation ; as, *e. g.*, by Cyprian—"*ut signaculo Domini consummentur*"—quoted in Potter on Church Government, p. 190.

and shall sit down with Abraham, and Isaac, and Jacob." So we hold that believers shall come from all the world.

((Matt. viii. 11.)

Sec. 17. Therefore we ought to fish well and diligently, as the Lord tells us when he says, "Follow me, and I will make you fishers of men;" and again he says by the Prophets, "Behold I send you many fishers and hunters, saith the Lord," &c. Wherefore there was urgent need that we should so set our nets that a vast assemblage and multitude might be caught to God; that there should be everywhere clergy to baptize and exhort a people who needed and desired it, as the Lord admonishes and teaches us in the Gospel, saying, "Go ye therefore and teach all nations, baptizing them in the name of the Father, and of the Son, and of the Holy Ghost, teaching them to observe all things whatsoever I have commanded you; and lo I am with you alway, even unto the end of the world;" And again he says, "Go ye into all the world, and preach the Gospel to every creature. He that believeth and is baptized shall be saved." "And this Gospel of the kingdom shall be preached in all the world for a witness unto all nations; and then shall the end come." And again, the Lord speaking by his prophet says—"And it shall come to pass afterward, that I will pour out my Spirit upon all flesh, and your sons and your daughters shall prophesy, your old men shall dream dreams, your young men shall see visions; and also upon the servants and upon the hand-

(Matt. iv. 19.)

(Jer. xvi. 16.)

according to the command of God,

(Matt. xxviii. 19, 20.)

(Mark xvi. 15, 16.)

(Matt. xxiv. 14.)

and the oracles of the prophets,

maids in those days will I pour out my Spirit;" (Joel ii. 28.) and in Hosea he says, "I will call her my people which was not my people, and have mercy on her that had not obtained mercy; and it shall come to pass that in the place where it was said unto them, Ye are not my people, there shall they be called the children of the living God." Where- (Hosea i. 10 and ii. 23.) fore, behold, how the Irish who never had the knowledge of God, and hitherto worshipped only idols and unclean things, have lately become the people of the Lord, and are called the sons of God.

Sec. 18. The sons and daughters of Scotic princes are seen to be monks[3] and virgins of Christ. And there was one blessed Scotic[4]

---

[3] *Monks.* St. Bernard, in his life of Malachy, written A.D. 1115, speaks of Ireland as a land "unaccustomed to monastic religion, and having never had any experience therein;" and, according to Malachy himself, it had "heard, indeed, the name of a monk, but had never seen a monk." This seems inconsistent with the words of the Confessio, but the meaning is, that those in St. Patrick's days were not properly monks, in the sense intended by St. Bernard, who judged them by the Cistercian Order, to which he belonged. The later monks were ordained and bound by vows of celibacy and poverty.— See *Bingham's Antiquities of the Christian Church*, Book VIII., chap. iii.

The dissolution of the monasteries and convents in England in the sixteenth century, and their restriction or total suppression throughout almost the whole of Europe in the nineteenth, bespeak the public sense of the evils which experience has shown to result from the present system.

[4] *Scotic.* Ireland was called Scotia, and the people Scots, until the eleventh century. "It was," says Bede, "properly the country of the Scots." (*proprie patria Scotorum.*) As to the origin of the name, Dr. Petrie observes, "The people of Ireland, according to all the Shanachies, were called Fenii,

G

maiden,[5] very fair, of noble birth, and of adult
age, whom I baptized, and after a few days she
came to me, because, as she declared, she had
received a response from a messenger of God,
desiring her to become a virgin of Christ, and to
draw near to God. Thanks be to God, on the
sixth day from that, she with most praiseworthy
eagerness, seized on that state of life which all
the virgins of God likewise now adopt, not with
the will of their parents, nay, they endure persecution and unfounded reproaches from their
parents, and nevertheless the number increases
the more ; and as to those of our kind[6] who are
born there, we know not the number, besides wi-
dows and continent persons. But those [virgins]
who are detained in slavery are the most severely
afflicted, yet they persevere in spite of terrors and
threats. But the Lord gave grace to many of my
handmaidens, for whether as much [as they
ought, or not,] they zealously imitate him.

Sec. 19. Wherefore, although I could have
wished to leave them, and had been ready and
most desirous to go into Britain, as if to my pa-

(marginal notes:) with such fruit that many men

(marginal notes:) and many virgins enter the monastic state.

Gael, and Scoti, from three of their celebrated progenitors."—
Tara Hill, p. 99.

[5] *Maiden.* This incident, which comes in so abruptly, is not
in the Armagh copy, and looks very like an interpolation ; it
is thought to have been inserted to favour the story that St.
Brigid was baptized by St. Patrick.

[6] *Our kind.* Those who were converted to the Gospel, and
born again of incorruptible seed ; namely, " by the word of
God, which liveth and abideth for ever ;" or, perhaps, those
who are natives of that country.

rents,[7] and country; and not that alone, but had He declares that he cannot leave the work which he has commenced.
been ready to go as far as Gaul to visit my bre-
thren, and to see the faces of the Lord's saints;[8]
God knows that I greatly wished it, but I am
"bound in the spirit," who "witnesseth" that if (Acts xx. 22.)
I do this he sets me down as guilty. I also fear
to lose the labour which I have commenced, and
yet not I, but Christ the Lord, who commanded
me to come and be with them the remainder of
my life. If the Lord willed it so, and guarded
me against "every evil way" [it was] that I
should not sin before him. I hope [to do] that
which I ought, but I trust not myself so long as
I shall be "in this body of death," because he is (Rom. vii. 24 —margin.)
strong who daily endeavours to subvert me from
the faith and chastity which I have proposed to
myself, even to the end of my life, to Christ my
Lord; but the carnal mind, which is enmity, although conscious of his own weakness.
always draws me to death—that is, to unlawfully
accomplishing desires; and I know in part why
I have failed to live a perfect life, as well as

[7] *Parents.* "As St. Patrick was far advanced in life at the time he wrote the Confessio, it seems more probable that the term *parentes*, in this passage, is to be understood, not of parents in the English sense of the word, but of relatives. This acceptation of *parentes* had crept into use as far back as the time of St. Jerome, and hence the Italian, *parenti*, and the French, *parens*."—Lanigan, *Eccl. Hist.* vol. i. p. 128.

[8] *Lord's saints.* "That he stood in peculiar connexion with the religious men of the south of France is evident from this passage."—*Neander.* It will be noticed that St. Patrick speaks in the text of Gaul as beyond Britain; and as he was writing in Ireland, it follows that the island of Great Britain is meant, and not Brittany, as some have thought.

THE CONFESSIO OF ST. PATRICK.

other believers ;[9] but I confess to my Lord, and I lie not, from the time that I knew him (that is, from my youth), the love, and fear of God increased in me—so that up to this time, by the grace of God, " I have kept the faith."

[9] *Sicut et cæteri credentes.* His meaning evidently is, " while conscious that all have sinned and come short of the glory of God, I am, through Divine grace, so acquainted with my own heart, as to be in some measure aware of the cause of my failure—to know the ' sin that does so easily beset me.' " That *credentes* means true believers here, we may gather from other passages—as, (ch. iii. sec. 12,) "*Deum vivum non credebam,*" which does not mean that he was a heathen, but a nominal Christian ; and again, (ch. iii. 14,) " *Ut eum sine fine crederem.*"

CHAPTER V.

HE DECLARES WITH HOW MUCH DISINTERESTEDNESS HE HAD PREACHED THE GOSPEL.

SEC. 20. Let him who pleases deride and insult me,[1] I will not be silent, nor will I conceal the signs and wonders which were ministered to me by the Lord, who knew all things many years before they existed, as it were "even before the world began," wherefore, I ought to give thanks without ceasing to God, who often pardoned my folly even out of place, and not in a single instance only; that his anger was not fierce against me, but that he granted me the privilege of being a labourer together with him, and I did not immediately acquiesce, as it had been pointed out to me, and as the Spirit prompted. And the Lord had compassion on me, among thousands of thousands, because he saw in me a readiness of mind. But I was perplexed as to what I should do about my condition, because many were endeavouring to hinder this mission, and were talking among themselves, behind my back, and saying, "Why does he endanger his life among

Entering on his missionary work after some delay.

---

[1] *Insult me.* "He seems to allude to a sort of murmuring against him, originating, it would appear, in a spirit of rivalry and jealousy, which actuated some of the Christians who were in Ireland before his mission."—*Lanigan*, vol. i. p. 285.

enemies, who know not the Lord ? " It was not
and, some-
what moved
by the objec-
tions of
others, with malicious intent they said this, but because
they did not approve of it, as I also understood (I
myself bear witness), on account of my imperfect
education. And I did not immediately recognize
the grace which was then in me ; but now I am
aware of what I should have known before.

Sec. 21. I have now, therefore, simply informed
my brethren and fellow-servants who have believed
me, why I have preached and preach still, to
strengthen and confirm your faith. Would that
you too may aim at nobler things, and succeed
better in them ; this shall be my glory, because
(Prov. x. 1.) "a wise son is the glory of his father." You
know, and God knows, how I have lived among
he declares
his integrity
among the
heathen, . you from my youth[2] up, faithful in truth, and
sincere in heart. I have also made known the
faith to those tribes among whom I dwell, and I
will continue to do so. God knows I have not
overreached any of them, nor do I design it, from
fear for the interests of God and his Church, lest
I should excite persecution for them and all of us,
and lest the name of God should be blasphemed
by me, because it is written, "Woe to the man by

---

[2] *Youth.* It is generally supposed that he came to Ireland
to preach the Gospel in the sixtieth year of his age. Whether
this was so or not, these words are no difficulty, as he may
refer to the six years of his youth which he spent in captivity,
when that great change was wrought in his heart which he
speaks of in the earlier part of the Confessio. At that period,
his piety and zeal for divine truth were as conspicuous as at a
later period of his life—a fact which he here appeals to their
experience to confirm.

whom the name of God is blasphemed;" for, (Lev. xxiv. though in all things I am unskilled, yet I have [16.]) endeavoured to be on my guard, even with Christian brethren and virgins of Christ, and religious women, who, of their own accord, used to bestow gifts upon me, and to place their ornaments[8] on the altar; but I returned them again to them,[4] and *and how he rejected* they were offended at me for doing this. But I *gifts,* was moved by the hope of immortality, to guard myself cautiously in all things, so that they should not find me unfaithful, even in a tittle, and that I should not give room to the unbelievers, even in the least, to defame or detract from the ministry or my service.

Sec. 22. But, perhaps, when I baptized so *and baptized,* many thousand men, I hoped to receive from some of them even half a scriptula?[5] Tell me, and I will give it back to you. Or, when the Lord ordained clergy by my weak ministry, did I *and ordained clergymen* confer that gift on them gratuitously? If I have *gratuitously,* asked of any of them even the value of a shoe,[6] (1 Sam. xii. 3.)

---

[8] *Ornaments.* Large numbers of golden ornaments, of various kinds, are constantly found in Ireland, which belong to a very remote period. Dr. Petrie notices two golden torques, found on Tara Hill, which cannot be of later date than the sixth century.—*Essay on Tara Hill,* pp. 181-184.

[4] *Returned them again to them.*—See this assigned as a reason for Secundinus' writing his hymn, p.

[5] *Half a scriptula—Dimidium scriptulæ.* The screapall was a coin used by the ancient Irish, which weighed twenty-four grains, and was of the value of three-pence.—*Petrie's Essay on Round Towers,* p. 214.

[6] *Calceamenti.* Like Samuel (1 Sam. xii. 3) and St. Paul, (Acts xx. 33,) he calls the people to witness his integrity and disinterestedness while among them.

tell it—tell it against me, and I will repay
it to you. I rather expended, whenever it appeared requisite, [money] for your sakes; and I
went among you everywhere for your sakes, in
constant danger,[7] even to those distant parts
beyond which there were no inhabitants, and
where no one had ever come to baptize, or ordain
clergymen, or confirm the people; [and] the Lord
assisting me, I adopted every means for your
salvation, using all diligence and zeal. And
during this time, I used to give rewards to kings,[8]
because I gave hire to their sons, who travel with
me; and thus they abstained from seizing me

suffering the with my companions. And, on one day, they
loss of his
own proper- desired exceedingly to kill me; but my time had
ty as well by
violence, not yet come, and they carried off everything they
found with us, and fettered me with iron; but,
on the fourteenth day, the Lord loosed me from
their hands, and whatever was ours was restored
to us, through the power of God, and by means
of the attached friends whom we had before provided.

Sec. 23. But you know how much I paid to

[7] *Danger.* His disregard of danger appears in the manner
in which he attacked the Druidic religion not long after his
arrival. (Introduction, pp. 19, 20.) On that occasion the
king was almost persuaded to be a Christian; but, as it frequently happens in the case of weak-minded and ignorant
people, he could not bring himself to leave the religion in
which he was born. "Niall, my father," he replied, "commanded me not to believe, but desired me to be buried on the
heights of Tara, like men in hostile array."—*Tirechan, quoted
by the Editor of the Book of Rights.* p. 225.

[8] *Rewards to kings.* See an instance in Introduction, p. 21.

those who were the judges,[9] through the districts that I more frequently visited, for I think I paid them the hire of fifteen men[1]—no small sum— that you might enjoy me, and I you, always in *as by liberal expenditure;* the Lord. I do not regret it, nor is it sufficient for me. I still spend, and, moreover, will spend. The Lord is able to grant me afterwards to expend even myself for your sakes. Behold, I call God to witness to my soul that I lie not, nor have I written to you to give you an opportunity of gratifying my love of flattery, or my avarice, nor that I might hope for honour from you. For sufficient to me is the honour which is not seen, but believed in from the heart; but the faithful One who has promised it never lies; and I see *(Heb. x. 23.)* that now, in the present world, I am exalted beyond measure by the Lord; but I was not worthy nor fit to be favoured by him, since I know most certainly that poverty and calamity suit me better than luxury and riches, and Christ *(2 Cor. viii. 9.)* the Lord also was poor for us. But, wretched and unhappy that I am, even if I wished for *preferring to be poor after* wealth, I now have it not; neither do I judge *the manner of Christ,* myself, [to want it,] because every day I disregard either the danger of being put to death, or over-reached, or brought into slavery, or of becoming

---

[9] *Judges.* "He means the Irish Brehons, or judges, who held their courts on the hills, and decided causes according to the Druidic laws."—*O'Conor.*

[1] *Fifteen men.* O'Conor thinks this refers to the eric, or pecuniary compensation for violating the law, or it may have been in the nature of a voluntary fine to secure the good will of persons whose influence must have been considerable.

a stumbling block to any one. But I fear none of these things, relying on the promise of the Heavens; for I have cast myself into the hands of the Omnipotent God, who reigns everywhere: as the prophet says, "Cast thy burden upon the (Psl. lv. 22.) Lord, and he shall sustain thee."

(1 Pet.iv.19.) Sec. 24. Behold, now I commit my soul to God, who is faithful, whose mission I perform, lowly that I am. But because he accepts not the person, and has chosen me to this office, that I alone, of the very least of his people, should be his minister, "What shall I render unto the (Psalm cxvi. Lord for all his benefits towards me;" and what 12.) shall I say, or what shall I promise to my Lord, for I see that I should have had nothing, unless he himself had given it to me; but I will search my heart and reins, because I am ardently de-for whom he sirous and ready that he should give me to drink desires to suffer any-of his cup, as he has granted to others who have thing, loved him. Wherefore, may God never permit that I should lose his people whom I have acquired in the ends of the earth. I pray God that he may grant me perseverance, and that he may vouchsafe to permit me to bear faithful witness to him, even unto my death. And if I ever effected anything good on account of my God whom I love, I entreat him to grant me this, that with those converts and captives I may pour out my even martyr-blood for his name, even though I should be de-dom, prived of burial, or my dead body be miserably torn limb from limb by dogs or wild beasts, or though the birds of the air should devour it. I

believe most certainly that if this should happen
to me, I have gained my soul with my body ; for
without any doubt we shall rise one day in the
brightness of the sun, that is, in the glory of
Christ Jesus our Redeemer, the Son of the living
God, "joint-heirs with Christ," and to be con- (Rom. viii. 17, 29.)
formed to his image, since of him, and through
him, and to him, we shall reign. For that sun (Rom. xi. 36.)
which we see, rises daily at God's bidding for us ;
but it shall not reign for ever, nor shall its
splendour continue, and woe to its unhappy wor- certain of the glory which
shippers, for punishment awaits them. But we is prepared for such
believe in and adore the true Sun, Christ, who persons.
never shall perish, nor shall he who does his will, (1 John ii. 17.)
but shall abide for ever, as Christ also shall abide
for ever, whose reign with God the Father
Omnipotent, and with the Holy Ghost, was in (Rev. xix. 6.)
the beginning, is now, and ever shall be. Amen.

Sec. 25. Behold again and again I briefly set
forth the words of my Confessio. I bear
witness in truth and joy of heart, before God
and his holy angels, that I never had any occasion, except the Gospel and its promises, to
return to that nation from which at first I escaped
with difficulty. But I pray those who believe in He repeats
and fear God, whoever may vouchsafe to look his Confes-
into or receive this writing which I, Patrick, the sio
sinner and unlearned, wrote in Ireland, that no
one may ever say, if I have demonstrated anything, however weak, according to the will of God,
that it was one so ignorant. But do you judge,
and let it be most firmly believed, that it was the

gift of God.　And this is my Confessio,[2] before
I die.

---

[2] *Confessio*—i. e., This is my declaration respecting myself, my life, my motives, and my teaching, which in the near
prospect of death, I place on record, for the use of the present
and future times.

THE EPISTLES OF ST. PATRICK.

BOOK II.

TO COROTICUS.

I, Patrick, a sinner and unlearned, declare[1] that I was made Bishop in Ireland. I most certainly hold that it was from God I received what I am, and therefore for the love of God I dwell a pilgrim and an exile among a barbarous people. He is witness that I speak the truth. It was not my wish to use language so harsh and severe [as in this letter,] but I am compelled by a zeal for God, and the truth of Christ, who stirred me up for the love of my neighbours and sons, for whom I have given up country and parents, and am ready to give my life also if I am worthy. I have made a vow to my God to teach the people, although some may despise me. With my own hand I have written and composed[2] these words to be delivered to the soldiers of Coroticus,[3] I

Inspired by zeal he sends this Epistle

---

[1] *Declare—Fateor*, whence *con-fiteor, Confessio.* In both letters the word is used in the sense of a declaration.

[2] *Written and composed*—Scripsi et condidi.

[3] *Coroticus*—He is supposed to have been the Caredig or Ceredig, son of Cynedda, who flourished in the fifth century, and who gave his name to the county of Cardigan in Wales. He appears to have been nominally, at least, a Christian.

say not, to my fellow-citizens,[4] nor to the fellow-
citizens of the Roman saints, but to the fellow-
citizens of demons, who, on account of their evil
deeds, abide in death after the hostile rite of the
barbarians ; companions of the Scots and apostate Picts,[5] desiring, as it were, to glut themselves with the blood of innocent Christians, multitudes of whom I have begotten to God and confirmed in Christ.

to rebuke the cruelty of Coroticus to the Chris-tians,   2. A cruel slaughter and massacre was committed by them on some neophytes, while still in
their white robes,[6] the day after they had been

[4] *My fellow-citizens—Civibus meis.* As this letter was written
in Latin, to be read to the soldiers, they must have been able
to understand it, and, therefore, were either Romanised Britons
or descendants of Roman colonists in Britain, either his fellow-
countrymen or Roman citizens ; but he repudiates their claim
to either title on account of their crimes. Some copies have—
" To the Christian subjects of Coroticus." It is evident,
however, that the object was to reach and influence Coroticus
himself.

[5] *Apostate Picts—Pictorum apostatarum.* The Pagan Scots
of Argyleshire, descended from an Irish colony, who (according to Dr. Todd) settled there in the third century, and
the Pagan Scots from Ireland, were long confederate with
the Picts against the Roman power in Britain. The term
apostate here is applied to the Southern Picts, whose
country lay southward of the Frith of Forth. They were said
to have been converted by Ninian, A.D. 412, according to
Bede, and probably only embraced Christianity nominally,
relapsing again into Heathenism. The Northern Picts, whose
territory lay beyond the Grampian hills, continued Heathen
until A.D. 565, when they were converted by the labours of St.
Columba.—See Reeves's Adamnan's Columba.

[6] *White robes.*—See Introduction, p. 24. The primitive custom of investing baptized persons with white robes, is not
now in use, though something of the kind is occasionally
practised at Confirmation. The reference here probably

anointed with chrism, and while it was yet visible on their foreheads. And I sent a letter by a holy Presbyter, whom I taught from his infancy, accompanied by other clergymen, to intreat that they would restore some of the booty or of the baptised captives whom they had taken, but they turned them into ridicule. Therefore I know not for whom I should rather grieve, whether for those who were slain, or those whom they took captive, or those whom Satan has so grievously ensnared, and who shall be delivered over like himself to the eternal pains of hell, for " whosoever committeth sin is the servant of sin," and (John viii. 44.) the child of the devil.

3. Wherefore, let every one who fears God know, that strangers to me and to Christ my God, whose ambassador I am, are parricides and fratricides, ravening wolves, " eating up the Lord's people as they eat bread," as he says, " Lord, the (Ps. xiv. 4.) wicked have made void thy law," with which (Psalm cxix. 126.)

includes Confirmation, as it was the custom in the fifth century to administer Baptism, Confirmation, and Holy Communion at the same time, not only to adults, but even to infants ! Thus Gennadius of Marseilles, A.D. 495, has the following passage in his treatise on Ecclesiastical Dogmas :—
" If they be infants that are baptized, let those that present them to baptism answer for them according to the common way of baptizing, and then let them be confirmed by imposition of hands and chrism, and so be admitted to partake of the Eucharist," chap. lii., quoted in Bingham, Antiquities of the Christian Church, Book xii. chap. i. sec. 2. The use of chrism in baptism, which has no authority in Holy Scripture, is rejected by the Church of Ireland; and infant communion is also rejected by her and the Church of Rome, though retained by the Greek Church.

Ireland had been in these latter days, most ex-
cellently and auspiciously planted and taught by
God's favour. I do not usurp another's rights,
but I have a share with those whom he called
and appointed to preach the Gospel amidst no
small persecutions, even to the end of the earth,
although the enemy grudges [us our success]
through the tyranny of Coroticus, who fears not
God, nor his priests, whom he has chosen, and
granted to them that most high and divine power,
that those whom "they bind on earth are bound

(Matt. xviii. in heaven."
18.)

recounting   4. Wherefore, I earnestly beseech those who
the threaten-
ings of Scrip- are holy and humble of heart not to be flattered
ture
by them, nor to eat or drink with them, nor to
receive alms from them, until they repent with
bitter tears, and make satisfaction to God, and set
free those servants of God and baptized hand-
maids of Christ, for whom He was crucified and
died. "The Most High rejects the offerings of
the unjust; he who offers a sacrifice from the
substance of the poor is like one who offers a son

(Ecclus.
xxiv.23,24.) as a victim in the sight of his father. The
riches which he has gathered unjustly shall be
vomited forth again; the angel of death drags
him, [away,] he shall be punished by the rage
of dragons; the tongue of the adder shall slay

(Job. xx. 15,
16,26.) him; unquenchable fire shall consume him."[7]

---

[7] Most of the texts quoted in the Epistle, and particularly
these, differ widely from the Vulgate, and are evidently taken
from one of the earlier versions ; but, in some cases, perhaps
the writer meant to give the substance only, and not the exact
words of Scripture.

And therefore " woe to them that fill themselves
with that which is not their own ;" or " what is (Hab. ii. 6.)
a man profited, if he shall gain the whole world (Matt. xvi. 26.)
and lose his own soul."

It were too long to enter into particulars, or
to enumerate one by one the testimonies from
the [Divine] law against such cupidity.   Avarice
is a deadly crime.[8]   " Thou shalt not covet thy (Exod. xx.)
neighbour's goods."   " Thou shalt not kill."   No
murderer can dwell with Christ.   " Whosoever
hateth his brother is reckoned a murderer." (1 John iii. 15.)
" He who loveth not his brother abideth in
death."   How much more is he guilty who has (1 John iii. 4.)

---

[8] *Deadly crime—Crimen mortale.*   The primitive Church
distinguished between sins of greater and less magnitude,
terming the former *crimen ;* the latter, *peccatum* (crimen est
peccatum grave, accusatione et damnatione dignissimum.—
Augustine.)   In this they followed Scripture (Psalm xix. 12, 13 ;
Luke xii. 47 ; Matt. v. 22, &c.)

They also described them as mortal and venial ; but in doing
so they never meant to deny that all sins are *in their nature
mortal ;* and accordingly, the early Christian writers, e.g.
Gregory Nazianzen, Basil, Jerome, Gregory the Great, and many
others, say, that there is no sin so small but that in rigour of
justice it would prove mortal, if God would enter into judgment with us, and be extreme to mark what is done amiss
against His law. (See Bingham's Antiquities of Christian
Church, book xvi., chap. iii., sec. 14.)

That this was St. Patrick's view is plain from his *Confessio,*
where, quoting the passage which St. Augustine frequently
refers to for the same purpose, " Every idle word that men
shall speak, they shall give account thereof in the day of judgment" (Matt. xii. 36), he goes on to say, " Therefore I ought,
in fear and trembling, to dread this sentence on that day when
no one shall be able to withdraw or hide himself, but all must
give an account even of the *least sins* (etiam minimorum pec-

stained his hands with the blood of the sons of
God, whom He has lately acquired in the very
ends of the earth, through my humble exhortations.

and his own
sacrifices.

5. Did I come to Ireland without the Divine
will, or merely from carnal motives? Who
compelled me? I am bound in the spirit not
to see my kindred any more. Do I show a
true compassion for that nation which formerly
took me captive? I am free-born according
to the flesh, for my father was a Decurio.[9]

catorum) before the judgment seat of Christ the Lord."—
Confessio, chap. i., sec. 3.

The Church of Rome, using the same terms (venial and
mortal), teaches a doctrine wholly different from this, viz.,
that "there is a whole kind of sins which are venial *in their
own nature*, such which if they were all together, all in the
world conjoined, could not equal one mortal sin, nor destroy
charity, nor put us from the favour of God." (Bp. Jeremy
Taylor, Diss., chap. ii., sec. 6, par. 3.)

This is distinctly opposed to Holy Scripture, which tells us
that "sin is the transgression of the law," (1 John iii. 4), *any*
transgression ; and "the wages of *sin* is death " (Rom. vi. 23).
"Cursed is every one that continueth not *in all things* which
are written in the book of the law to do them." (Gal. iii. 10.)
See also Matt. v. 19, xii. 36.

The primitive usage survives in the Book of Common
Prayer, as in the Litany, " From all other *deadly* sin ;" it also
occurs in the XVIth Article, but is disused in other parts
of these formularies, as liable to misconception. Ancient
modes of expression and usages, however harmless in their
original intention, are sometimes wisely laid aside, when their
meaning has been perverted.

[9] *Decurio.* The office of a Decurio was that of a magis-
trate and counsellor in the Roman colonies. In later times
the clergy were exempted by law from these offices ; but in
the times here spoken of, and in the remote colony to which

I have bartered my nobility for the good of others. I am not ashamed, nor do I repent of it. In short, I am delivered over in Christ to a foreign people for the unspeakable glory of the eternal life, which is in Christ Jesus our ·Lord, although my own friends do not acknowledge me. "A prophet has no honour in his own (John iv. 44.) country."

Are we not of one fold—have we not one father? as the Lord says, "Whosoever is not with me is against me, and he who gathereth not with me scattereth." It is not fitting that (Matt. xii. 30.) "one should destroy and another build." Do I (Eccles. xxxiv. 28.) seek my own?

6. Not to me, but to God be the praise, who put into my heart this anxious desire, that I should be one of the hunters and fishers[1] whom God long since foretold should come in these last days; I am envied. What shall I do, Lord? I am greatly despised. Behold, thy sheep around me are torn and pillaged by the aforementioned robbers, by the orders of Coroticus; our enemy. Far from the love of God is he who delivers Christians into the hands of the Scots and Picts.

the father of St. Patrick belonged, there is no difficulty in believing him to have been at the same time a Deacon and a Decurio, especially as he is represented as having had some landed property in the colony.—Todd, St. Patrick, p. 354, note.

[1] *Fishers—Piscatoribus.* See Confessio, chap. iv., sec. 17, where the passage from Jeremiah is quoted. To a people in the earlier stages of their career, thinly scattered through a country abounding in game, few figures would be more expressive than this.

Ravening wolves, they have devoured the Lord's flock, which was increasing rapidly in Ireland with the utmost diligence; and the sons and daughters of Scotic princes[2] were becoming monks and virgins of Christ in greater numbers than I can tell. He who incurs thy displeasure by his oppression of the righteous, shall abide under it for ever.

7. Which of the saints would not shrink from partaking of the sports and banquets of such men. They have filled their houses with the spoils of the Christian dead. They live by rapine; they know not mercy; they drink poison; they reach the deadly food to their friends and children, like Eve who knew not that she was giving death to her husband. It is the custom of the Roman and Gallic Christians to send men of holy life, and fit for the office, to the Franks[3] and [other]

[2] *Scotic Princes.—Filii Scottorum ac filiæ Regulorum.* See Confess., chap. iv., sec. 18. It has already been mentioned that two races are spoken of in St. Patrick's letters as dwelling in Ireland : the Scoti, who were the rulers, and the Hiberionaces, or Hiberneginæ, who composed the mass of the people. The latter are named from the country, which he always speaks of as Hiberio. The Scoti were a colony from Spain, who, according to the Irish bards, settled in Ireland in the year 1000 B.C., led by the sons of Golam Miled, i.e., the Miles, or Knight, from whom they are popularly called Milesians.

[3] *To the Franks—Ad Francos.* The Franks, who invaded and conquered Gaul, and from whom it derives its modern name of France, did not embrace Christianity until A.D. 496, and therefore this Epistle, which speaks of them as still Pagans, must have been written before that date.

foreign people, with many thousand shillings,[4] to redeem baptized captives. You who so often kill them, or sell them to a foreign people ignorant of God, delivering over the members of Christ, as it were, to infamy, what hope have you in God?

8. Whosoever consents with you, or uses words of flattery to you, God will judge, for it is written, "Not only they who do evil, but they that consent thereto are to be condemned." *He sympathises with the victims,* (Rom. i. 32.)

I know not what more to say or to speak, of the sons of God who are dead, slain with the sword, for it is written, "Weep with them that do weep;" and again, "If one member suffers, all the members suffer with it." Wherefore the Church weeps and laments her sons and daughters whom the sword of the enemy has not slain, but who have been carried away to far-off lands, where sin openly prevails and shamelessly abounds. There Christian freemen are sold and reduced to slavery, and that by the most unworthy, most infamous and apostate Picts. Therefore, I will cry aloud with sorrow and grief; O most goodly and well-beloved brethren and sons whom I have begotten in Christ without number, what shall I do for you? I am not worthy to aid the cause of God or men. The unrighteousness of the unrighteous has prevailed against us. We are become as *(Rom. xii. 15.) (1 Cor. xii. 26.)*

[4] *Solidi.* The solidus was a gold coin originally worth twenty-five denarii, but in the time of St. Patrick it was reduced to one-half its value, and was probably worth from seven to eight shillings.

aliens. Perhaps they do not believe that we have received one baptism, and have one God and (Eph.iv.5,6.) Father. With them it is a crime that we were born in Iberia,[5] but it is said, Have ye not one God, why do ye wrong one to another? Wherefore I grieve for you; I grieve, my well-beloved, for myself, but at the same I rejoice that I have not laboured in vain, and that my pilgrimage has not been in vain. A crime has been committed which is horrible and unspeakable. Thanks be to God, ye, O believers and baptized ones, have departed from the world to Paradise. I behold you. Ye have begun your journey to that region[6] where there shall be "no night," nor

[5] *Iberia.* This passage is very obscure, and according to the Bollandists, defective. The MSS. differ very much. Some read "de Hibernia" (of Ireland,) and if this is the true reading, we must understand him as speaking in the person of his Christian people. The translation of Dr. Todd is followed here, but he offers no suggestion as to the meaning of Iberia. The Bollandists think that "some one who is more happy at guessing than they are, may make sense of the passage."

[6] *Region.* It will be observed that he regards the departing Christian as passing from earth to heaven direct. So St. Paul (Philippians i. 23) says, "I am in a strait betwixt two, having a desire *to depart and to be with Christ;*" and again, (2 Cor. v. 8), to be "absent from the body," is to be "present with the Lord." So, in the well-known hymn :—

> " There is a land of pure delight,
>   Where saints immortal reign,
> Where endless day excludes the night,
>   And pleasures banish pain ;
> There everlasting spring abides,
>   And never-withering flowers ;
> *Death, like a narrow sea, divides*
>   *That heavenly land from ours.*"

"sorrow," nor death any more, but ye shall re- (Rev. xxi. 4, 5, 25.) joice as "calves let loose, and ye shall tread down (Mal. iv. 3, 4. the wicked, and they shall be as ashes under your feet."

9. Ye therefore shall reign with the Apostles, and contrasts their happy and Prophets, and Martyrs, and shall receive an lot everlasting kingdom, as He himself bears witness, saying, "They shall come from the east and from the west, and shall sit down with Abraham and Isaac and Jacob, in the kingdom of heaven." Rev. xxii. 15.) "Without are dogs, and sorcerers, and murderers, and liars, and perjurers, whose part shall be the lake of fire eternal." For not without reason does the Apostle say, "If the righteous scarcely be saved, where shall the ungodly, and the sinner, and the transgressor of the law be found?" (1 Pet. iv. 18 Where shall Coroticus be with his wicked rebels against Christ? Where shall they find themselves, who distribute among their depraved followers, baptized women and captive orphans, for the sake of a wretched earthly kingdom, which passes away in a moment like a cloud, or smoke scattered by the wind? Thus shall sinners and deceivers perish from the face of the Lord, but the righteous shall feast continually with Christ, and judge the nations, and rule over unjust kings for ever and ever.

10. I bear witness before God and his holy with that of their oppres- angels, that it shall be as my ignorance has said. sors. These are not my words, but those of God and the Apostles and Prophets, who have never lied, which I have put forth in Latin. "He who believeth

shall be saved, and he who believeth not shall be
(Mark xvi.
16.) damned." God hath spoken.[7] I earnestly entreat
whatever servant of God is willing to be the
bearer of this letter, that it may not be kept back
from any one, but may rather be read before all
the people, and in the presence of Coroticus himself.

But oh that God would inspire them, that at
some time they may return unto Him, that thus
even though late they may repent of their evil
deeds. They have murdered the brethren of the
Lord. But let them repent and release the
baptized women whom they have already taken
captive, that so they may be worthy to live unto
God, and may be made whole here and for
eternity. Peace be to the Father, and to the Son,
and to the Holy Ghost.[8] Amen.

---

[7] *God hath spoken—Deus locutus est.* We hear a different
formula now-a-days from this. The new style is, " Rome has
spoken ;" but St. Patrick knew no authority to appeal to but
that of God speaking in His word.

[8] This seems a singular doxology ; perhaps the author meant
gloria, or else we must take it as a prayer that Coroticus on
his repentance may have the peace of God. Todd, 385, note.

ST. PATRICK'S HYMN.

i. I bind[1] myself to-day to a strong virtue, an
   invocation of (the) Trinity.
   I believe in a Threeness, with confession of an
   Oneness in (the) Creator of (the) Universe.

ii. I bind[2] myself to-day to (the) virtue of Christ's
   birth with his baptism,
   to (the) virtue of (his) crucifixion with his
   burial,
   to (the) virtue of (his) resurrection with (his)
   ascension,
   to (the) virtue of (his) coming to (the) Judgment of Doom.

iii. I bind[3] myself to-day to (the) virtue of ranks (Lo. 1. 16)
   of Cherubim,
   in obedience of Angels,   (Heb. 1. 14.)

[1] *Atomriug* for *ad-dom-riug*; the verb *adriug* is equivalent
to *alligo*, "I bind to," with the personal pronoun *dom*. me,
infixed. This Hymn is written in a very ancient dialect of the
Irish language, of which we have proof in these infixed pro-
nouns which have ceased to be used for the last five hundred
years.

[2] The acts or events in our Lord's history noticed here are
seven in number; see verse vi. where the number of perils i
also seven.

[3] This verse, enumerating the servants of God in heaven
and earth, has the same thought as the collect for St. Michael's
day, in which God is said to have " ordained and constituted

(Rev. xxii. 9.)   [in service of Archangels,]

(Acts xxiii. 6; Heb. vi. 19.)   in hope of resurrection for reward,

(Gen. xviii. 23-33.)   in prayers of Patriarchs,

(1 Pet. i. 12.)   in predictions of Prophets,

(Matt. xxviii. 19, 20.)   in preachings of Apostles,

(Acts vii. 55-60.)   in faiths of Confessors,

(Matt. xxv. 1-13.)   in innocence of holy Virgins,[4]

(Matt. v. 16.   in deeds of righteous men.

iv.   I bind[5] myself to-day to the virtue of Heaven,
In light of Sun,
In brightness of Snow,
In splendour of Fire,

the service of Angels and Men in a wonderful order." We have also in the former part a parallel to the words of the Trisagion in the Communion service, "With Angels and Archangels, and all the company of heaven."

[4] *Inendgai noemingen.* Archdeacon Hamilton, P.P., in the Summary of the "Life of St. Patrick," p. 6, prefixed to his translation of the *Confessio* (Dublin, O'Reilly, 1859), translates this line, "The purity of the holy Virgin"! which of course suggests to most readers that the Virgin Mary is intended. Was this an oversight? He must have been aware that St. Patrick never once mentions the Virgin Mary, nor does Secundinus, which is certainly inconsistent with the veneration of her as now practised in the Church of Rome.

[5] The heathen Irish deified the powers of nature, as appears from the case of King Laeghaire, (Leary,) who, being taken prisoner in battle, "swore by the Sun and Moon, the Water and the Air, Day and Night, Sea and Land, that he would never demand the Borumean tribute again;" but having broken his promise, "the Sun and Wind killed him."—See Annals of the Four Masters, A.D. 457, 458. St. Patrick, as a Christian, claims to have them all on his side.

In speed of Lightning,
In swiftness of Wind,
In depth of Sea,
In stability of Earth,
In compactness of Rock,

v.   I bind myself to-day to God's[6] Virtue to
         pilot me,
     God's Might to uphold me,
     God's Wisdom to guide me,
     God's Eye to look before me,
     God's Ear to hear me,
     God's Word to speak for me,
     God's Hand to guard me,
     God's Way to lie before me,
     God's Shield to protect me,
     God's Host to secure me,
     Against snares of demons,[7]
     Against seductions of vices,
     Against lusts of nature,
     Against every one who wishes ill to me,
     Afar and anear,
     Alone and in a multitude.

vi.   So have I invoked all these virtues between
         me, [and these]

---

[6] This enumerates some of God's attributes.

[7] In these lines the spiritual enemies of the Christian are noticed—"the devil, the world, and the flesh." The following appear to refer to the bodily dangers which were at this time present to his mind.

against every cruel, merciless power[8] which
    may come against my body and my soul
against incantations of false prophets,
against black laws of heathenry,
against false laws of heretics,
against craft of idolatry,
against spells of women and smiths and
    druids,
against every knowledge that defiles men's
    souls.

II.[9]

VII.   Christ to protect me to-day,
        Against poison, against burning, against
        drowning, against death-wound,
        Until a multitude of rewards come to me!

[8] The belief was universal among the primitive Christians
that behind the heathen systems of the world, and operating
through them, there were demons, who "were still permitted
to roam upon earth, to torment the bodies and to seduce the
minds of sinful men." St. Patrick, no doubt, shared in this
belief, and therefore, in the great contest at Tara, he was not
without apprehension, from the incantations of the Druids.

[9] The second part seems to be a working out of the promise
of Christ (Matt. xxviii. 20) in the fullest detail. In stanzas
vii., viii., ix., He is invoked no less than sixteen times, an
emphatic commentary on 1 Tim. ii. 5—"There is one God,
and one mediator between God and men, the man Christ
Jesus." This invocation harmonizes with the Creed in the
Confessio, by the prominent position which it gives to the
Second Person of the Trinity.

VIII.   Christ with me, Christ before me, Christ
       behind me, Christ in me!
    Christ below me, Christ above me.
    Christ at my right, Christ at my left!
    Christ in breadth, Christ in length, Christ
       in height!

IX.   Christ in (the) heart of every one who
       thinks of me,
    Christ in (the) mouth of every one who
       speaks to me,
    Christ in every eye that sees me,
    Christ in every ear that hears me!

X.   I bind myself to-day to a strong virtue, an
       invocation of (the) Trinity.
    I believe in a Threeness with confession
       of a Oneness, in the Creator of [the
       Universe.]

    Salvation is the Lord's, salvation is the
       Lord's, salvation is Christ's.
    May Thy salvation, O Lord, be always
       with us.[1]

[1] In the original, these three concluding lines are in Latin.

SECUNDINUS'S HYMN OF ST. PATRICK

TEACHER OF THE IRISH.

AUDITE.

Hear all ye who love God, the holy merits
Of the Bishop Patrick,[1] a man blessed in Christ ;
How, on account of his good actions, he is likened unto
    the angels,
And for his perfect life, is counted equal to the Apostles.

2 Cor. xi. 5.

BEATI.

He keepeth the commandments of the blessed[2] Christ
    in all things,
His works shine brightly before men,
Who follow his holy and admirable example,
Whence also they glorify the Lord his Father which is
    in heaven.

John xiv. 15; Matt. v. 16.

---

[1] *Patricii.* "Patrick, i.e. nomen graidh le Romanu, i.e. the name
of an order among the Romans," (G.) ; meaning the Patrician Order.

[2] *Beati Christi . . . mandata.* The Book of Hymns reads *beata*—
i.e., the blessed commandments of Christ.

CONSTANS.

Steadfast in the fear of the Lord, and immovable in
faith ;
On whom, as on Peter,[3] the Church is built ;
Who received his Apostleship from God.[4]
The gates of hell shall not prevail against him.

1 Cor. xv. 58 ; Gal. i. 1 ; Matt. xvi. 18.

DOMINUS.

The Lord chose him to teach the barbarous nations,[5]
To fish (for men) with the nets of doctrine,
To draw believers from the world unto grace,
That they might follow the Lord to the heavenly seat.

Matt. iv. 19.

[3] *Super quem ædificatur ut Petrum ecclesia.* The reading in the Book
of Hymns is *Petrus*, and the meaning then would be "on whom the
Church, like Peter, is built." The commentary is as follows :—" When
it is said, Thou art Peter, and on this rock I will build my Church,
it is interpreted, Peter *acknowledging* [Christ.] Matt. xvi. 16 ; whosoever therefore desires to enter into the kingdom of heaven must acknowledge God by faith like Peter " G. According to this note, Peter
is addressed, not in his personal, but in his representative capacity, as
a "confessor of Christ," and thus others, share his privilege. The
Church, in fact, is "built on the foundation of *the Apostles* and
Prophets, Jesus Christ himself being the chief corner stone," (Eph. ii.
20,) and St. Patrick, according to the author, as another Apostle, takes
his place with St. Peter and the rest. In a certain sense, as the note
seems to intimate, all Christians partake of the honour as "living
stones," 1 Peter ii. 5.

[4] *Cujusque apostolatum a Deo sortitus est,* or "the Apostleship of which
(i.e. the Church) he received from God." "*Cujusque,* i.e. *Ecclesiæ,*"
Todd, *Book of Hymns ;* but this seems doubtful. Here, as in the
Confessio, he ascribes his coming to Ireland to a divine call.

[5] *Barbaras,* "i.e. foreign, because foreign to the Roman language."
G. Ireland never having formed part of the Roman Empire, and not
speaking the Latin language.

ELECTA.

He trades with the choice Gospel talents[6] of Christ,
Which he puts out at usury amongst the Hibernian
nations,
Destined hereafter, along with Christ,[7] to possess the
joy of the heavenly kingdom,
As a recompense for this labour.[8]

Matt. xxv. 14-30; John xiv. 3.

FIDELIS.

A faithful minister and distinguished messenger of God,
He shows to the good an apostolic example and pattern ;
Who preaches to the people of God, as well by deeds as
by words,
So that by good works he may provoke those to imita-
tion, whom he does not convert by his words.

1 Tim. iv. 6, 12.

GLORIAM.

He has glory with Christ, and honour in this world,
Being venerated by all as the angel of God ;
Whom God sent, even as Paul,[9] to be an Apostle to the
Gentiles,
To guide men unto the kingdom of God.

2 Tim. i. 11 ; Gal. i. 1.

---

[6] The talents of Christ mentioned in the Gospel.]

[7] *Cum Christo.* As the Lord says in the Gospel, " Where the carcass
is there will the eagles be gathered together ;" as if he said distinctly,
" Where Christ in the flesh shall be, there shall the just be also, and
thus shall they be always in heaven with Him." G.

[8] *Navati hujus laboris.* The reading in the B. of H. is *navigii*,
that is "the voyage of the Church ;" here "the sea is the present
world ; the ship is the Church ; the pilot is the preacher (*forectlaid*)
who brings her to the port of life; the port is the life that is perpetual." G

[9] *Ut Paulum.* " As Paul was sent to the Gentiles, so Patrick was
sent to the nations of the Scoti (Irish)" G. Here there is evident

HUMILIS.

Humble, through fear of God, both in spirit and be-
haviour,
Upon whom on account of his good actions rests the
Spirit of the Lord :
Who beareth in his righteous flesh the marks of Christ,
In whose cross alone he glories and sustains himself.

Gal. vi? 14-17.

IMPIGER.

He diligently feedeth believers with heavenly food,[1]
Lest those who are seen with Christ should faint by the
way :
To whom he distributes the words of the Gospel like
the loaves
In whose hands they are multiplied like the manna.

Matt. xv. 32; Exod. xvi. 14-18; John vi. 11.

KASTAM.

Who, through the love of God, keepeth his flesh pure,
Having prepared it to be a temple for the Holy Spirit,
By whom it is constantly possessed with good motions ;
And who offers up his body a living sacrifice, well-pleas-
ing to the Lord.

John iii. 3; 1 Cor. vi. 19; Rom. xii. 1.

---

reference to St. Paul's description of himself as "an Apostle, not of
men, neither by man, out by Jesus Christ and God the Father," Gal.
i. 1.

[1] *Dapibus*—"of his preaching." G. There is in this verse a double
reference ; to the manna in the wilderness, and to our Lord's miracles.
Of the accuracy of this description there can be no doubt, as the
writer, from his intimate association with St. Patrick, must have been
familiar with his preaching.

LUMEN.

He is a great and burning evangelical light[3] of the world,
Set upon a candlestick, shining unto the whole world ;
A strong city[3] of the king, set upon a hill,
In which is much store of the riches of the Lord.

John v. 35 ; Matt. v. 14, 15.

MAXIMUS.

He shall be called the greatest[4] in the kingdom of heaven
Who fulfils, by good works, what he teaches in his holy
    discourses.
He goes before with a good example, and a pattern to
    the faithful ;
And in a pure heart has faith towards God.

Matt. xviii. 1-3 ; 1 Tim. iii. 9 ; iv. 12.

NOMEN.

He boldly preaches the name of the Lord to the Gentiles,
To whom he gives the eternal grace of the laver of sal-
    vation ;

----

[3] *Lumen.* " Lux is the element itself— lumen what issues from the lux ; that is, the brightness." G. The meaning of this note, probably, is that St. Patrick shone with a light derived from Christ, and thus was only in a secondary sense a light of the world.

[3] *Civitas.* St. Patrick, not the Church, is here compared to a forti- fied city of a king, set on a hill, which, with all its treasure, is the king's property. " The fruitful hill is Christ." G.

[4] In the legendary account of the origin of this hymn, it is said that St. Patrick, when he heard the hymn recited, not knowing at the time to whom it referred, the first verse having been omitted, objected to this word ; but an explanation was offered that *greatest* was put for *great.* The gloss explains it by *peroptimus,* the very greatest.

For whose offences he daily prays to God :
For whom also he offers up sacrifices[5] worthy of God.

Acts ix. 29; Jas. v. 16; Phil. iv. 18; Heb. xiii. 15, 16.

OMNEM.

He despises all the glory of the world, in comparison
    with the Divine law,
Counting all things as but chaff, compared with Christ's
    table ;[6]
Nor is he disturbed by the violence of the thunder of
    this world ;
But rejoices in tribulation when he suffers[7] for Christ.

Phil. iii. 8 ; Acts. v. 41.

PASTOR.

A good and faithful shepherd[8] of the Gospel-flock,
Chosen by God, to watch the people of God,
And to feed, with Divine doctrines, the nation ;
For which, after the example of Christ, he is giving his
    life.[9]   *John x. 14; xv. 13; xxi. 15.*

[5] *Hostias ;* "that is, spiritual sacrifices." G. "Sacerdotium sanc-
tum offerre *spirituales hostias.*"—1 Pet. ii. 5. Vulgate.

[6] *Mensam.* This line in the Book of Hymns is, *Que cuncta ad cujus
mensam estimat cisciliam.* The Irish note interprets *mensam* "*men-
suram,*" i.e., measure ; and then the passage will run, "He despises
all the glory of the world in comparison with the Divine law, measured
by which he also estimates all things as chaff."

[7] *Patitur.* "He suffers for Christ, who denies himself and takes up
his cross daily." G.

[8] "He is a good shepherd who is like Christ, who says, I am the
good Shepherd, and lay down my life for my sheep." G. Confess.
chap. iv., secs. 16, 24.

[9] "As the Apostle says, "For I could wish that myself were accursed
from Christ, for my brethren, my kinsmen according to the flesh."—
Rom. ix. 3. G.

QUEM.

Whom the Saviour advanced for his merits, to be a
    Bishop,
That he might exhort the clergy in the heavenly warfare;
To whom he distributes the bread from heaven, along
    with garments,
Which is fulfilled in his divine and holy discourses.

          1 Tim. i. 18; John vi. 11; Matt. xxii. 11.

REGIS.

A messenger of the king, inviting believers to the mar-
    riage,[1]
Who is arrayed in the wedding garment;
Who draws the heavenly wine[2] in heavenly vessels,
Pledging the people of God in the spiritual cup.

                  Matt. xxii. 2.

SACRUM.

He finds in the sacred volume a sacred treasure,
Which he purchases with his holy and perfect merits.
He discerns also the Godhead of the Saviour in the
    flesh.
He is named Israel,[3] beholding God in his spirit.

          Matt. xiii. 44; Gen. xxxii. 28, 30.

---

[1] The allusion would seem to be to the marriage feast, Matt. xxii. ;
but the gloss quotes Luke xii. 36, "Be ye like unto men that wait for
their lord, when he will return from the wedding; that when he
cometh and knocketh they may open unto him immediately."

[2] "The wine of the doctrine of the Gospel." G.

[3] This refers to an interpretation mentioned by St. Jerome, in which
Israel was said to mean, *vir aut mens videns Deum*, "the person or
mind seeing God;" but the true meaning is, "a Prince with God."

TESTIS.

A faithful witness of God in the Catholic[4] doctrine,
Whose words are seasoned with the Divine oracles,
So that they are not corrupted, like human flesh, and
    eaten of worms ;[5]
But are salted with a heavenly savour for the sacrifice.[6]
Mark ix. 48-50; Col. iv. 6.

UERUS.

A true and excellent cultivator of the Gospel field,
Whose seeds are seen to be the Gospels of Christ,
Which he sows from his divine mouth in the ears of the
    wise,
And tills their hearts and minds with the Holy Spirit.
Matt. xiii. 1-9; Mark iv. 14.

[4] "Catholic means universal." G. We have here the primitive meaning of the word Catholic, as explained by Vincentius of Lerins, (Introduction, p. 33, note,) and as used by the Church of Ireland at the present day. Thus, in the Prayer for all Conditions of Men, the words are—" We pray for the good estate of the Catholic Church, that it may be so guided and governed by thy good Spirit, that all who profess and call themselves Christians may be led into the way of truth." In the Litany, " That it may please thee to rule and govern thy Holy Church Universal in the right way;" and again, in the Apostles' Creed, "I believe in the Holy Catholic Church." The Church of Rome wishes to be called the Catholic Church, but this is equivalent to saying that a particular Church is universal, which is a contradiction. It is sufficient to say that the claim is rejected by the great Eastern Church, and all the Reformed Churches, in other words, by the greatest and most highly civilized nations of the world. Here was the place for some mention of Rome ; but there is none, either in text or commentary.

[5] *Vermibus;* "that is, of knowledge." G. The meaning appears to be, that his words will be found so perfectly in accord with Holy Scripture, that no learning will detect any error.

[6] *Ad victimam.* In order that they may prove an acceptable offering.

XRISTUS

Christ chose him to be his vicar[7] on the earth,
Who liberates captives from a two-fold bondage;
And of the many whom he has redeemed from the
    bondage[8] of men,
Releases numberless persons from the dominion of the
    devil.   *Isai. lxi. 1; John viii. 31.*

YMNOS.

He sings Hymns, with the Apocalypse, and the Psalms
    of God,
On which also he [discourses,[9] for the edification of the
    people of God;
Which Scripture he believes, in the Trinity[1] of the sacred
    Name,
And teaches the One substance in Three Persons.
                         Rom. xv. 4.

---

[7] *Vicarium* means a "steward, or taxgatherer, or successor, (*com-orba*) for this is what Jerome says in his Epistle concerning the ranks of the Romans, that the vicar is the man who is instead of the count (*comes*) over the city, until the count or *comes* returns from the king," G. Thus here the king is God, the *comes* is Christ, the vicar is Patrick; but there is no such passage as that quoted, in the genuine works of St. Jerome. The reader will note that in Irish estimation St. Patrick was a vicar of Christ.

[8] See Epistle to Coroticus.

[9] *Tractat.* This is explained "*imluadid,* i.e., he puts in motion, announces, publishes." G. This line appears also in the Hymn of Fiacc. "Hymns and the Apocalypse, the Three-fifties (Psalms) he used to sing them;" and in the note there, the Hymns are explained to mean, the Te Deum, or, this of Secundinus. The exact meaning of *tractat* is, 'he handles or treats of.'

[1] *Credit.* "It is a great thing that he believes the law of the sacred name, which is the Trinity," G. It has been remarked as strange that there is no mention of the Arian Controversy in St. Patrick's works, but the manner in which the Divinity of Christ is dwelt on, and the sequent mention of the Trinity, appear to refer to it indirectly.

ZONA.

Girt with the girdle of the Lord, by day and night,[2]
He prays without ceasing to the Lord God,
Receiving the reward of which great labour,
He shall reign with the Holy[3] Apostles over Israel.

*Isaiah xi. 6; Eph. vi. 14; 1 Thes. v. 17;
Matt. xix. 28.*

[2] "Augustine says, If every day one observes fixed times of practising [prayer,] he prays without ceasing," G.

[3] *Sanctis.* Another reading is *sanctus,* i.e. "He shall reign with the Apostles, a saint over Israel," "that is, over those souls who see God," G. The meaning appears to be that St. Patrick holds a rank. equal to that of our Lord's twelve Apostles, and shall hereafter enjoy the same privileges. We have already seen that he is assigned the same position by the author as St. Peter and St. Paul. A later tradition of the Irish was that he should "judge the Scoti [Irish] at the day of judgment, as the Apostles were to judge Israel." This is founded on a legend given by Probus in his Life of St. Patrick, and is only referred to here as illustrating the strong Nationality of the Irish Church, which indeed is everywhere apparent throughout its early history.

Porteous & Gibbs, Printers, Dublin.

www.ingramcontent.com/pod-product-compliance
Lightning Source LLC
Chambersburg PA
CBHW022338020726
47500CB00004B/1175